Also by Robert Davis

That Girl
of Pierre's

Robert Davis

Illustrated by Lloyd Lózes Goff

BETHLEHEM BOOKS   •   IGNATIUS PRESS
Bathgate   San Francisco

© 1948 by Robert Davis

Cover art © Lydia Halverson
Cover design by Theodore Schluenderfritz

First Bethlehem Books printing February, 2007

ISBN 978-1-932350-14-2
Library of Congress Control Number: 2006935956

Bethlehem Books • Ignatius Press
10194 Garfield Street South
Bathgate, North Dakota 58216
www.bethlehembooks.com
1-800-757-6831

Printed in the United States on acid-free paper

To

JOY

NOELLE

KATHLEEN

ELISABETH

four girls of Arsac-le-Petit

who made it easier to understand

DANIELLE

Contents

1. *Wayfarers with a Two-wheel Cart*

EMPTY of all other travelers, the limestone ribbon of highway unwound behind and before the handcart. Danielle, hardened from months of this wandering, pushed the cart with quick, light steps: they were nearing home. Her little brother, with his hand touching hers on

1

the handle, was trotting to keep pace, and the sheep dog under the cart strained in her harness as she too sensed the long journey's end. In the cart, birdlike old Grandmother Mathilde was perched on the roll of bedding, her eyes intent upon the horizon.

"It will be along in here, Grandmère, that we'll see the steeple," Danielle encouraged. "I remember our last sight of it was from here in the woods of Cantemerle, a little after we crossed the Lorina."

She wondered whether Jeannot remembered how during that troubled flight from the enemy they hastily took a farewell glance at their beloved village of Arsac-le-Petit. "The steeple will be sticking up like a needle, thin and black, Jeannot, remember?"

The small boy shook his head.

His grandmother tried to help him: "Yes, like a needle out of a pincushion made of plane trees—it looks like that, Jeannot, remember?"

Again he shook his head and turned up his playful smile. Still playful, thought Danielle, and braver than he knew. He'd been game all the time. Maybe it was just as well he didn't remember the horror and sadness of that long-ago day.

"Danielle, let him come into the cart," Grandmère suggested softly. "Come, my Jeannot, stand up here and let your eyes be the first to see the steeple of Ste. Philomène."

He leapt upon the cart and stood as high as he could. His eyes suddenly widened. "There it is!" he cried shrilly, pointing. "There! And just like a stick, over that cornfield."

The hands of the two women groped for and gripped each other, and their eyes were moist.

"Now I can believe we are to see our home again," Grandmère said.

"And stay a long time?" Jeannot asked.

"Yes, little one," said Danielle, "and not sleep in barns and haystacks."

The sun was high, not quite noon, but they had been on the march since five o'clock, and accustomed though they were to holding their hunger, and eager to be there at last, she didn't consider it a wise plan to enter Arsac-le-Petit without having eaten something beforehand. There was no telling what ruins and sorrow they might need strength to face when they'd get there. "Let's eat here," she said, and guided the cart into a cluster of acacias, where an amber thread of water entered a culvert.

She spread a square of canvas on the ground, lifted the old woman down, and took a loaf of bread and a round of cheese from a cloth wrapping. "As for you, Jeannot, fill the bottle at the stream, but do it before you stir the mud with your feet. I will not untie Bergère until you have finished." The tongue in the dog's wide-open mouth was already curling to taste the water.

The grandmother drew a clasp knife from her pocket, and hugging against her bosom the loaf of bread, long and solid

as a small log, she turned it round and round as she cut off slices. "Eat to your hunger, my children. Our last meal as homeless wanderers. Today we need not economize. Home again in Arsac, we will not skimp on food, not with the good credit we have at the store." Her voice was comfortable and comforting.

She settled her back against a tree. "These last two weeks of vagabondage I thought would never end," she sighed. "And it has been wearing on you, my Danielle. You are a brave girl. God is kind to have given me such a grand-daughter. But these hardships have made you as flat as a cracker. I want to see my granddaughter look more like a woman, rounder. Thin as you are, you have much beauty, with your black hair and your quiet eyes, so serious for your young age. But I don't think those at home will be glad to see you so thin."

Those at home! There had been no definite news of the girl's mother and father for three appalling years. But Danielle refused to believe them dead. Surely some man of Arsac, some returning prisoner or demobilized soldier, might have news of them. The war had been full of coincidences; and now on every hand you heard of people drifting into contact with friends, persons who had been reported dead reappearing alive as ever, families reuniting. Was there any good reason for not thinking the Dufours wouldn't have their turn too? . . . And Marc. Never for an instant through all the troubles she had experienced had her feeling for him wavered. But she had schooled herself not to let her missing him burden her mind. It had been necessary for each of the three, she and Grandmère Mathilde and little Jeannot, to keep up a brave front, one for the other, so that even now she could, ever so softly, hold Marc back from her thoughts.

"Not tonight, but surely tomorrow night," Grandmère said, patting her hand, "I will have a thick, nourishing soup for you. And what a soup! It will be my masterpiece. It will have onions, cabbage, and carrots, a spoonful of fresh fat, and if they can be found, green peppers and tomatoes."

The sun filtered warmly through the foliage as they ate their road rations. Danielle stretched her tired muscles, slipped off her sandals, and rubbed the hot soles of her feet, which at once felt soothed from having a little shady air around them. Things could feel good: surely there was good awaiting them at home. Bergère, dripping from her wallow in the stream, retreated a distance and took to biting at her hard chunk of bread as though it were a soup bone. Insects droned overhead.

First the brother, then the grandmother yawned, nodded, pillowed their heads on their arms; they dozed comfortably, with the ease of long practice. Leaving them to their nap, Danielle went down the slope and let her feet luxuriate in the brook. The foamy feel of the current and the rustling noises of the water and the trees seemed like promises of clean new strength for the tasks ahead. And she would need strength, trying to take her parents' place.

Her father had joined the army at the very first of the war. The following spring her mother had heard a rumor that he was in a prison hospital near the Luxembourg frontier, and had set out to find him. She had become caught in the whirlpool of invasion, had been put into a labor battalion, and later shipped to the east. After that, no news. That was all.

Danielle let her eyelids close, to shut out the brilliance of the sky, she told herself; but it was also the pain of her recollections. In a little while they would be back in Arsac.

But who would be there to greet them? Neither her missing parents, nor Marc, nor Ovide, Marc's father. Curly-haired Ovide, her father's oldest friend, always ready for a frolic with the children—he'd been killed the first month.

She remembered a day like this one, a blue, windless day four years before, when the two fathers had gone rabbit hunting and taken her and Marc along to hold the dogs. After lunch they were all lying on the ground, the men smoking, she rubbing Bergère's ears, Marc untangling burdocks from Lion's fluffy tail—when the fathers had brought up the matter casually, without premeditation. But their words had made a new universe for Danielle and Marc.

"They look well together," her father had said.

And Ovide had mused, "A likely couple."

Then both men had nodded soberly.

"She will have the Dowry Field," her father had added.

"And he will have forty rows of vines, a yoke of oxen, and farming implements."

Thereupon both fathers, Ovide and Pierre, had agreed that Marc and Danielle should make out well enough with that to start them out in life together. And she now remembered how Marc and she had looked at each other then, smiling, both surprised and glad, overhearing so splendid a gift being planned for them. They had played together as far back as they could remember, probably even when they'd been infants in the crawling stage, before they'd even learned how to talk. And on that blue-sky day four years ago, it had seemed that their good, reliable fathers had promised them they'd go on playing together forever. She had been barely thirteen at the time. Neither Marc nor she was much of a talker, but each knew wholly how the other felt. There was a warm contentment in being near each other. They two, out of all the world, belonged together.

How soon after that both fathers had gone into the army, together, departing by the same train. Now Ovide was dead, Pierre's whereabouts unknown. And where, where was Marc? Perhaps she should have tried to keep him from enlisting, but when the father had been killed, the son had insisted upon taking the older man's place. Marc was well grown and had easily lied about his age. No stopping him.

She sat up, rubbing her eyes. "What a stupid one I am to be dreaming like this, wasting time so nearly home!" She scrambled up the slope, repacked the cart with its homeward load, and called the sleepers as she briskly wheeled it into the road.

With the lively cheerfulness of elderly people when they are doing exactly what they wish, the grandmother was instantly astir, clapping her hands; but Jeannot was still dreamy-drowsy, and his big sister had to lift him upon the bed roll. "Finish your nap in peace, little one," she laughed.

Over the highroad she trundled her passengers, and a mile beyond the Lorina brook, they came to a height of land from which there was another view of Arsac-le-Petit. But this glimpse was so intimate and real that they had to stop and let a prayer of thanks well up from their hearts while their eyes took in the forgotten beauty of the scene.

Grandmother Mathilde sighed contentedly. "Many a time, my child, I doubted my old feet would ever stand again upon the Hill of Windmills and see this. There is no place like one's own."

At the foot of an undulating slope lay a huddle of rus-set roofs, each one the shelter of a lifelong neighbor. Yet now, after long absence and suffering in strange places, the women could, almost, look upon the village with the eyes of strangers. How gracefully the slender spire rose up from the midst of those houses and pierced the sky!

In another moment the cart was rattling down the home-ward slope of its own weight, and Danielle had to restrain rather than push it. Along the road were the rows of grape-vines and patches of plowland which furnished the food for the small community. But these fields, once tidy under crops of oats, potatoes, and sunflowers, were now waist-high with weeds. Vivid plumes of pine seedlings, of broom and of gorse, like battle flags, flaunted nature's reconquest of the soil man had abandoned. Only traceries of green upon the parched turf marked the stubborn remnants of vines which had not yet surrendered.

Mathilde's mood changed at the sight of the desolation. "Oh my beautiful vines! Does war kill vines as it kills vine-yardmen? Could no one raise a hand to save them? Never did I think to see them so forlorn." The old woman's grief was as personal as though she had lost human friends. "Never did I think to say what I now say. I rejoice that my Jules is not alive to witness this misery upon his land. The genera-tions of men who labored to make it fruitful, now all their work gone for nothing! It was Jules' pride to keep the alleys between the vines neat like the top of a table. And I worked beside him, as proud as he." Tears muffled her voice.

Danielle was silent. She was equally moved, and if she herself were given to words these would be the same feelings that she'd express. And so her grandmother's voice was, for the time, as her own.

"You hear men say, 'This land belongs to us,' but it is not so. We belong to the land. Men are born, are here for a day and are gone, but the land remains. It is forever here, willing to feed us if we do our part. But if man does not obey the law of the land he starves." Mathilde raised her arms and let them fall helplessly, the immensity of her thought dwarfing her powers of expression.

"But what would you, Grandmère?" Danielle tried to reason. "I feel as you do, but who has been at fault? For more than three years here, there have been no men, no horses, to do the plowing. No sulphur, no lime or copperas, to prevent mildew. No hands to prune away deadwood, to hoe and burn the witchgrass from the roots. None to cut the suckers that steal the blood of the plant. Isn't it wonderful enough, then, that the brave old things still show a spark of green?"

It was quite a speech, and she felt almost as if she were addressing the dead and dying vineyards of the valley, reassuring them that help was now on the way. "We are only two, Grandmère, but that's at least two. Soon Jeannot will be big enough to help, and we shall be three—until the others return . . ." She stopped talking as they approached the village.

Quivers of heat swam upward. Canvas curtains hung limply in the doorways. The good people of the bourg, protected by their masonry walls and their solid shutters, were still at their mid-day slumber. In fact, Jeannot too was still drowsing in the cart.

What a small grey town to have seemed so warm in their memories! Shabby now, neglected, disorderly. The wood of the doors and the windows showed grey beneath flaking paint. Roofs grey under crusted lichens. Gardens grey under undisturbed dust. Dust on thistles and ragweed. Dust, dust. And greyness.

Mathilde and Danielle, in mute agreement, sank to the ground in the shade of the plane trees. Here they were, in the triangular Place de la République, the center of their Arsac-le-Petit. But this desolation made them loth to go too directly to their own house and see its ruin, or seek out too soon the townfolk, those who might be here. So they felt torn by conflicting emotions. Of course it was good to be home, and yet the village as they found it somehow affronted them. It was as though Arsac had deceived them. During their travels they had held up their heads, had even boasted a little, as befitted citizens of no mean neighborhood. But now returning from wide travels, and having had an experience of imposing cities, the paltriness and untidiness of Arsac became something like an insult. The Place de la République, why, it was no more than the intersection of three rutted roads. Not more than a dozen of the thirty dwellings (come to think of it, now) had a third room. Only two houses had a second story. And, look, how the awning over the Café des Trois Moulins hung in rags, its outdoor tables paintless, its windows grimy!

Jeannot, waking at last, sat up in the cart. "Is this Arsac-le-Petit?"

"Yes, little cabbage." Danielle tried to cushion the shock. "You're home at last."

"Huh, it's little and dirty. I guess they're pretty poor around here."

"But it's our home," the old woman said sternly. "I was born here and so were you both. It's ours, small as it is and shabby, it's ours."

"And we love it," said Danielle sharply in self-reproof for her own disparaging judgment of the moment before. Then, almost as a reward, the modest beauty of the church of Ste. Philomène, to which her back had been turned, met her glance. Its sculptured porch invited one to rest from the world's sorely traveled roads and to know grace. Yes, the church-side of the Place was still lovely, just as their memories had treasured it: the tower the loftiest in the canton, and its bell, if anyone were still here to ring it, the most sonorous in tone. And Father Ambrose the best-loved priest in the department. Was he still alive? Ah, in a short while, when the few people who might now be in Arsac would awake, they would learn everything. Meanwhile, this brief glance at Ste. Philomène had renewed their courage to face the worst, if they must.

She roused her tired muscles, knowing how much wearier was the grandmother. "Come, Grandmère," she said, lifting her gently by the elbow, "we shall see what we shall see."

"Yes, enough woolgathering," agreed the old woman. "We're going home."

The boy and dog had set off upon explorations of their own around the Place, but now came hurrying back. "Everybody's gone or is still asleep," Jeannot said wonderingly. "Is it always like this?"

"No, little brother," Danielle said, running her hand through his sunburned hair, "there is much life here."

As they walked on, passing house after house, the two women named in their minds and sometimes aloud the inhabitants of each, mimicking their accents and peculiarities. Here, within a few feet of them, might be sleeping the carpenter, there the storekeeper, yonder the lawyer and the priest. There was the house of Agathe Bracessac, Marc's grandmother. One glance at its disrepair, and they knew that he had not yet returned. They clasped each other's hands the tighter and braced their shoulders a little more. There was the house of Odette Bosc, robe and mantle-maker. In the next lived Marisma, Mathilde's life-long friend. And over there was the home of Vivette, who had been like Danielle's twin to her. She, her mother, and grandfather had taken flight on the same panicky morning as Mathilde and her grandchildren had. But Vivette had gone south, not east. Maybe by now they had returned; the house looked open. Danielle curbed an impulse to run over and see. Home came first.

Their own house, when they at last pushed the cart up to it, was still closed. Clearly, Pierre and Jeanne had not returned.

"Where are our father and mother?" the boy asked, staring about in dismay.

"We've beaten them home, Jeannot," said Danielle, trying to keep the disappointment out of her own voice.

Beside the door a huge sunflower, sown by the wind and watered by the drip from the eaves, stood silent sentinel with its golden face. A banksia rose bush, which had been a pet of Danielle's since childhood, had pushed its tendrils across the front of the cottage, as though to seal it from strangers.

"Jeannot," the grandmother commanded, to snatch him from grieving, "fetch our key from the woodshed. What, you've forgotten? It will be hanging on a nail under the big bench. Make haste."

When Jeannot returned with the key, Danielle found she had to bend the branches of the rose bush aside in order to get the key into the lock. "One good old friend at least," she said gaily, "is here to hand us a bouquet at the threshold. A good sign!" She pressed a fragrant cluster against her cheek.

The two-wheel cart was home from its travels.

2. *Nesting In*

WITHIN the kitchen, save for the film of dust and the damp spots on the floor, all was as they had left it many months before. The rush-bottom chairs against the wall, the table black with age and cookery, the tumbled beds, old Mathilde's brushwood broom and sabots in the corner, the turkey-wing in the chimney, all were eloquent of the panic-driven morning of their flight.

Considering that the house had been uninhabited for two winters the weather had done surprisingly little damage. Near the ridgepole of the kitchen was a leak, probably a tile displaced by the wind. The rafters of the windowless chamber, where the grandmother used to mature her goats' milk cheeses, had rotted and fallen inward.

The old woman's first act was to wind the clock, looking out the doorway to take the hour from Ste. Philomène's steeple. Next she tiptoed circumspectly to the stable. In a stall she scuffed aside the straw and lifted a board. She was smiling broadly when she re-entered the kitchen. "I've always contended that a hole in the ground is the safest bank," she crowed. Opening a newspaper parcel she exhibited a string of gold beads, a cameo breastpin, and ten silver spoons.

"One thing more and my mind will be quiet. Come, Danielle, we must taste the well." She let the chain rattle through the overhead pulley, hauled up the dripping bucket. "Mmmm, sweet as clover. What water! Nowhere on our travels did we find water so living. My great-grandfather, who dug the well, said it was fed by an underground spring. It never runs dry. It's a blessing to have water like that in our dooryard."

Danielle's initial gesture as a housekeeper was to fling wide the windows and shutters for the sun to burn away the musty smell. She carried chairs into the courtyard and spread pillows and mattresses upon them. Jeannot, having sauntered through the rooms, promptly disappeared. Already he was enough of a man to flee when domestic chores threatened.

Immediate duties out of the way, the woman and the girl brought chairs into the shade of the Carolina poplar beside the well, the agreeable spot where the summertime meals of the family were eaten. "Let's take stock of what work is most pressing," said the girl, "and what means we have of getting it done."

"First and foremost, what cash money have we?" The grandmother was counting bills and coins out of her knitted purse. "Four hundred and twenty francs. Not very much, but we will stretch it out by using it only for the baker, for our day-to-day bread. Of more importance is our credit at the storekeeper's, the thousand francs he did not have when we sold him our cow and goats. With care that credit will cover our purchases for three months. We should accomplish much in three months. The way is clear, my Danielle, for you to give your whole attention to the vines, without anxiety for the housekeeping."

The currant bushes and fruit trees had survived, but the vegetable garden was a tangle of goldenrod and wild carrot. "As soon as we can find a man with a horse," Mathilde planned, "we will get that plowed. It is late in the season but I can still plant salads and winter greens. And there is the matter of chickens and rabbits! I entrusted Marisma with a rooster and eight hens when we left. Unless her character has changed she'll have something to put in our hen house." The old woman's morale mounted as the number of her projects multiplied. It was her nature to be as busy as a bird dog. Without effort she was already slipping back into the ruts of a lifetime. "And rabbits. I farmed out a full dozen. They'll be another dividend to collect. While you work the vines, my part will be the housekeeping, the garden, and the barnyard animals."

Mathilde attached a black sateen apron about her middle, inserted her feet into her sabots, and clumped off to inform her little world of her return. Jeannot was still away and Danielle was glad of the solitude. She was bone-tired after their long trek with the two-wheel cart, and would have welcomed a rest. She was a prudent girl and did not minimize the arduousness of the field work that she would soon undertake. The cutting and burning of weeds and the hoeing around the vine roots she could do by hand. That was woman's work. But for the deep plowing between rows they must find a man with a horse or with oxen, a man who would accept Danielle's handwork for his pay. In the tool closet she found what instruments she would need, and blessed her orderly father for leaving them sharp and in good condition. In the woodshed were about three hundred faggots and about as many oak logs—enough firewood to carry on with.

As she circulated through the buildings, planning ahead for her work and the family's well-being, she had an agreeable feeling of competence and self-assurance. She was growing up. She was taking her place in the Dufour family procession: craftsmen and custodians of vineyards. The resurrection of an ancient industry, as Marc would say, was at stake. And she had a part in it.

The idea lifted her above feeling much importance in her usual small personal tasks. Maybe it was foolishly ambitious of her, a girl of not quite seventeen, single-handed to put a whole farm into working order. But she did not even think to ask herself if she wasn't a little afraid to tackle so big a job. It needed doing too badly.

But not this very minute. What she wished to do most of all right now was to run up to Vivette's. If Vivette were at home, she'd be as good as the gossip columns of a newspaper—and she might have news of the missing three, Jeanne and Pierre and Marc. Danielle hastened indoors, washed her face, and smoothed her hair.

She was just setting off when a bicycle bell sounded in the street. Vivette! Vivette herself came running around the house! With rapturous squeals the girls fell into each other's arms.

"My dear, oh my dear, are you really back!" bubbled Vivette. "Now Arsac will be a different place. Oh, how I have missed you! And you'd never guess in a thousand years how I knew you were back. Your dog. My mother saw her out of the window and said, 'Isn't that the old dog of the

Dufours sniffing around the pig's pail?' And sure enough! I jumped on my bike. Oh, Danielle!" They clasped each other again, laughing and sobbing, smiling and weeping: Danielle tall, big-boned, thoughtful, with a mane of black hair; Vivette chubby, always on the verge of laughter, impulsive and blonde. Danielle usually said less than she meant and Vivette said more. They contrasted each other prettily. Yes, there had been little misunderstandings now and then back to the time they had sat together on the double bench in grammar school, but none of long duration. Each found sheer enjoyment in the company of the other.

"Come inside," said Danielle, wanting to play hostess already, with Vivette as her first guest. She was home, now. She had a home!

She was puzzled, though. "But, Vivette, you speak as though you'd been here a long time. You left the same day as we did. Where have you been all these months?"

"Why, right here in Arsac, except for the first week."

"Didn't the invaders bother you?"

"Not a bit. We needn't have been afraid at all. If we'd known what was on their minds, none of us need have run away." Vivette laughed at Danielle's incredulous look. "You see, it was like this. After we'd been running away for two days, Grandpère rebelled. You know how cranky he can be. Well, he said he was an old man and the few years he had left didn't matter. If he had to die he was going to die in his own bed. Next thing we knew, he was gone. It gave us the second big fright in two days. We looked all over for him, and surely enough we found him back home, living like a king in his own house."

"But the foreigners—?"

"Ah, you forget—we all forgot—what a reputation our

grapes have. Foreigners adore our red wine, especially these invaders. They wouldn't have hurt the vineyards for the world because they wanted them for themselves. Well, as I say, there we found the soldiers giving Grandpère potatoes and even tinned meat. So we stayed too. And when they left, they went in such a hurry they had no time to spite the vines."

As they chattered away about everything they had seen and thought and felt while apart from each other, they did not neglect the housework crying to be done. Mathilde's linen was aired and her bed made smooth with it. Windows and crockery washed. Cooking utensils scoured with sand. They talked on every subject but one, Marc. Of Danielle's parents no news, and so there was little to say. And she hesitated to bring up Marc's name first. Not that there was any secret about the feeling that she had toward him—least of all a secret from so close a friend as Vivette—but she felt that if it was good news Vivette would have blurted it out at once. Vivette gossiped freely enough about Ovide and Agathe Bracessac, but not a syllable about Marc. Was she holding something back? Sparing Danielle the worst until later? Once Danielle led the conversation up to Marc, and Vivette bluntly changed the subject. Her reticence was deliberate. It gave Danielle a tense pale feeling within. What was being held behind the laughing blue eyes of this dear friend who had always shared every confidence?

Outside the window and door was a great noise: quacking ducks and the rumble of a wheelbarrow announcing Mathilde's approach. Jeannot was pushing the barrow, upon which were enthroned a drake and two ducks, a rooster and six pullets, four cabbages, five heads of lettuce, a peck of potatoes, and a topping of onions and carrots.

But before she so much as greeted Vivette the old lady had to relieve her mind. "I want to apologize, first thing I do, to Arsac-le-Petit. My first impressions were false. It's not much to look at, it's down at the heel and grubby, but the people! They are the best-hearted on earth. And I've had the promise of six rabbits as soon as they are old enough to wean. Well, what have you two been up to?"

By this time the house was almost back to its normal order, a change that seemed incredible to the grandmother for two such chatterbox girls to have effected in the time since she'd stepped out on her foraging. The dust was gone, kitchen things gleamed. The house already had a lived-in smell. Shadows from the candle and the fire flickered on the walls.

The hour was so late that Vivette was persuaded to stay for supper.

"No soup tonight," the grandmother sighed, "but to-morrow Marisma's bringing up some peppers and I'll get a square of pork from the store. Mmh, Mmh!" The girls laughed, for the old lady's vanity as a soup-maker was a neighborhood byword. For her no meal was worthy of the name which did not center about a steaming casserole. "My Jules swore that he could tell my soup among a thousand. And, my children," she brought her voice down to a confiding whisper, "in twenty years the men never guessed that I simmered four leaves from the laurel bush, out there, in with the onions!"

"I'm pinching myself, dear people, to make sure I do not dream," Danielle said, standing between her grandmother and her friend, a hand on the shoulder of each. "We are at home and our friends have not forgotten us. I have a feeling that Pierre and Jeanne are even now making their way toward us—" Marc's name was on her tongue, but she checked herself.

In the grandmother's mind a festive idea was replacing her regrets about a soupless first supper at home. "Let's celebrate anyhow." She carried a lighted candlestick into the cheese room, and pointed to a ring in the trapdoor. The girls lifted out the wooden square and let down the ladder from the cheese room. Then both climbed down, in response to instructions.

"Scuff your feet in the far corner," the old woman called down to the mystified girls as she held the light over the black hole. "There should be four bottles. My father put ten of them there the year I was born."

Surely enough, Danielle's toes found them, and Vivette selected one, hugging the dusty old bottle close for fear of accident.

"Aha, that's it!" Grandmère exclaimed. "The wine of baby's year, my blessed father called it—when I was a baby just born." She seemed almost like a quaint infant now, in her bliss. "There were ten, but life so far has called for six: my engagement, then my marriage, and the baptism of the children. And now if this isn't a day to celebrate too, I don't know what is."

Over their cheese and bread and salad they drank in little sips, after making a ceremony of it, pledging good fortune to the living, peaceful repose to the dead, naming each beloved by name. They wished speedy homecoming for the wanderers. "And a speedy reunion also," Mathilde said, smiling at her granddaughter, "of lovers."

Danielle smiled back, but out of the corner of her eye watched Vivette, who applauded, but said nothing. The supper went on, Grandmère pouring into her own glass what remained of Jeannot's wine after the few sips he was allowed. It was something almost sacred with them, the fine wine of their district, the end-product of endless toil and loving care of the vines, and something never to be abused or wasted. And this vintage tonight was especially precious, drop for drop.

Vivette at last kissed them each on both cheeks, then mounted her bicycle and was gone. The grandmother and the girl sat on, the table between them, both in deep thought, the one living in her past, the other in her future. The boy drowsed over his bread and milk, and the old dog whined in her dreams.

Vivette probably knew something, thought Danielle, and had some dire reason for concealing it. Could Marc have become involved in some disgrace? No, no, why think such a thing? Or interested in some other girl?

Danielle wondered whether she should mention her anxiety to Mathilde, ask her if she hadn't also noticed how Vivette had not said a word about Marc? Or maybe the grandmother knew and was trying to save her pain?

Then, over Arsac-le-Petit flowed the mellow music of Ste. Philomène's bell tolling the Angelus. The notes quivering in the air seemed as caressing as the twilight.

She and the grandmother rose and crossed themselves, their lips moving. They had wandered far in fear, and now they were in their own home again, inexpressibly weary, but before them was a night of rest in real beds. Tomorrow would be their first whole day at home. Then Danielle would demand to be told. Until then she would let the peace of this hour sustain her.

3. *Porky Guichard's Lie*

TO DANIELLE the interval between waking and getting up was one of the most delicious moments of the day. Rested and warm between the sheets, she floated in a cloudland of irresponsibility. No duties weighed upon her. The day was not yet born. There was time to arrange her thoughts. And this morning she could do so in her own village, her own home, her own bed.

She had slept like a graven image, and was on the point of opening her eyes when Ste. Philomène struck five. Mathilde had not budged and Jeannot was breathing like a young steam engine.

But she did not wake with an entirely untroubled mind. The riddle that she had taken to bed still nagged her. What was Vivette's secret about Marc? It was too stupid, both to have doubts about Marc and to have concealment between herself and Vivette. She resolved that the day should not end until she had learned what her friend was hiding.

Next door a hammer was pounding an anvil. Victor was early at his forge. The blacksmith and his wife, Blanche, had been away from home the previous evening and the Dufours had missed them. If Victor was stirring she would catch him before he left. Inch by inch, she eased herself from under the covers, dressed, and went out into the dewy freshness. What a wonderful thing is a night! It winds up the clock of our energy. It sets us going with enough vitality to last until another nightfall.

The smith stared at her and laid aside his hammer. "Blanche," he shouted toward the living-quarters. "Come see who's here. Come a-running."

His wife opened wide her arms and kissed the girl soundly. "My dear, I am rejoiced to see you. We were speaking of you only yesterday. Do you bring news of your parents?" Danielle shook her head and the three stood in disappointed silence.

The girl addressed the blacksmith directly. "And how is business with you, Victor?"

"I can't complain. There's no end of work, if I had the metal. But they don't ship us iron any more. Plow points, for example. Here am I, up at cockcrow, hammering a makeshift plowshare out of the tire of an old cart wheel."

"Good," said Danielle. "That fits in well, because I came to talk business. Over at our house some tiles have blown loose on the upper course, and in Mathilde's cheese-room seven of the rafters have rotted and caved in. To replace the rafters we can hew young pines in our wood lot, and Pierre has a stack of salvaged tiles behind the barn. All I need is a workman. You are clever with your hands, Victor, and I hoped you might be willing to help us." The smith made a face of humorous resignation.

"We haven't a lot of money," pursued the girl, "and I've been thinking how we can pay you. Father was forehanded. Hanging under the harness are three new plow points. If we furnish the material for the roof and you do the work, would the points pay you?"

The man was studying the firm, strong features of the girl. "Sew up your pockets, Blanche," he said to his wife. "Our innocent little Danielle went away, but it's a horse trader who has come back. But yes, that exchange suits me. Lately I've put my hand to about every trade, and I might as well add roofing to the list. You bring the points over and I'll get at your roof this afternoon. Just the same, it isn't for the points alone that I am doing this. I like your spirit. It isn't every girl who would start in to resurrect a farm, single-handed, before breakfast, on her first morning home."

Danielle shook hands with the smith, kissed his wife again, but in the doorway she paused and turned. "You ought to know the horses hereabouts. Is there a man with a sound horse but a bad harness?"

"That's not hard to answer, as there are actually but six horses in the commune. Felix Dassier still has his big roan mare. She sidestepped the draft because she was nursing a colt. But last week his horse collar broke smack across the hinge. The leather tore like paper."

Victor would have said more, but with a thank-you and a wave of the hand the girl was gone. "Keep your eye on that girl of Pierre's," he said to his wife. "She's smart and getting smarter."

Felix was unlocking the padlock of his barn when Danielle came round the corner of his house. "By St. Christophe," the fat man cackled, "I didn't know you were within a thousand miles of here. Pierre is with you?"

The girl shook her head. She inquired into the health of the Dassier family, then became more objective. "I think we have a nice job for you. To plow our 'Thirty Rows' piece of vines. How much will you charge for it, and when do you think that you can get at it?"

Felix's face was a comic blend of anxiety to please, of sales resistance, and of resigned refusal. "I'd like nothing better, Danielle, but right now I couldn't plow a window box. I broke my collar and there isn't a harness maker nearer than Bordeaux."

"Would you plow it if you had a collar?" she persisted.

"Of a surety I would. I'd do it today, and it wouldn't cost you much either. I'm terribly sorry."

Danielle had entered the stable and was measuring the roan with her eye. "Do you think the collar of Pierre's black would fit her? If it's too large you could pad the top with a folded sack. If you can make it work, I'll give you the collar for plowing our vines and garden, if you will do it within the week."

Felix began to hedge. "Well, that is to say, I'll be glad to do it sometime. But I'm terribly behind in my work. I'll try to get it done in a couple of weeks."

"Have it your own way," interrupted the girl crisply. "But you yourself have been complaining that the mare can't leave the barn as things are. Let's compromise. You bring the mare along to our house and we'll try the collar. If you can use it, you plow our Thirty Rows today, and the garden and the rest of the vines next week. Does that sound fair?"

The teamster already had his horse untied. "We'll make it fit, you and I." He chuckled to himself, half in amusement, half in admiration, as Danielle left for home.

Breakfast was never more than a brief, hasty bite among

Arsac householders, by reason of the fact that men and women alike worked in the fields from dawn till dark. Supper was the real forum for the discussion of family affairs. It was a relaxed and dilatory meal, the principal distraction in a laborious day. Young and old would mull over the cheese and the pitcher of piquette until it was time to tumble into bed. No one was disposed to wash the supper dishes. Breakfast, as a consequence, would consist of a bowl of warm milk for the children, and a bowl of coffee-and-milk for the adults, supplemented by whatever broken meats remained overnight upon the table. The menfolk having finished the chores around the barn, and having sharpened their tools for the day, would eat standing in the doorway, one ear receptive to the conversation in the kitchen, one eye upon events in the street and the impending weather. The women would consume their morning beverage as they swept, washed up, made the beds, got the ingredients for the midday soup into the pot. Then they would go out and follow the men into the field.

Mathilde and Danielle sauntered about, coffee in one hand, bread in the other, while the girl recounted her two pre-breakfast bargains.

"I don't like it. You make it sound too good," was the old woman's flatly adverse comment. "Things don't come that easy. It's been my experience that the devil puts you off your guard before he sets his mischief on you. I'm superstitious that way."

The grandmother had rested well and was in high spirits. "I'm making a trip to the store this morning, and it's a scene that I've lived through a hundred times. This time Porky Guichard is in my debt! It's enough to make me feel like a duchess. I'll buy what I want and just wave my hand.

'Write it down in the book, if you please, against my credit of a thousand francs.' Oh, la, la, won't the eyes of the other women pop out!"

They were still eating when the bell of Vivette's bicycle tinkled. "I just had to run over to make sure you were really here. You can't guess how lovely it is to be able to drop in and say hello whenever I feel like it. I didn't realize how much I was missing you. It starts the day right."

She stayed only a minute, and there was not time nor the privacy to corner her about Marc.

With her saw-tooth hoe across her shoulder, Danielle told Mathilde: "Take Jeannot with you to the store to carry the basket. And have the soup hot and lots of it. I'm going to follow right behind the plow while the earth is soft. And as for you, young Jeannot, no monkeyshines. No falling out of trees, no throwing stones at the swallows that have young ones in the barn."

As Mathilde imagined it, her first appearance at the general store would be like the coming-out reception of a debutante. Customers, she expected, would crowd about to shake hands. They would ply her with questions: Had she seen their second cousins who lived in the Midi? What changes in Arsac-le-Petit had she noticed? What did she think had happened to Pierre and Jeanne? The old lady rehearsed her entry. She rearranged her hair, encasing the knob in a piece of black foulard.

Her progress across the Place, her entry into the store and the questioning were as she had anticipated. But if she had been shocked the previous day by the shabbiness of Arsac's external appearance, the drabness and scantiness of Guichard's merchandise sent her heart into her boots. Even the heartiness of the greetings could not counteract the depression of those empty shelves. Where were the bulging stocks of three years before, the hams hanging from the ceiling, the festoons of sausage, the sprightly packages of spice and soap, the pyramids of canned fruits and vegetables, the sober cartons of sugar and sweetened cookies, the wooden cases of figs and prunes and apricots?

Mathilde packed the salt, coffee, lard and salad oil into her basket. Then, not to be deprived of her big scene, said to Porky, "Write it down in the book, if you please. It will be a deduction on the thousand francs you owe me."

The stout storekeeper regarded her coldly. "What thousand francs is that, Grandmère?"

She supposed at first he might be teasing her. She smiled.

"Listen to him," she said, looking at the customers and jerking her head toward him, " 'What thousand francs?' he says."

Guichard took a deep breath and put on such a poorly acted look of surprise that she laughed outright. "Why," she said, "the thousand francs that you did not have right by you when you bought my cow and goats, that last morning, the day everybody hurried away from here? Come now, surely you remember it?"

Guichard stared, without expression or sound of reply. No, he wasn't joking.

Mathilde, fear chilling her heart, began frantically to add details. "Surely, you couldn't forget *that*? The store was full of noisy people. Families were buying supplies and collecting their children. Carts crowded the street. It was a shamefully small price that you offered, but what would you, we had heard the cannon that morning. You said you had only a thousand francs in your pocket for the moment, but for us to drive the animals into the courtyard and to come back in an hour for the other thousand. We came back, the girl, the boy and I, but you had stepped out. We waited two hours, as long as we dared, but you didn't return. You *must* remember. And now that we are back we'll take the balance that's due in trade, if it's the same to you."

Guichard still stared with his near-together piggy eyes. "I remember none of it. The cow and the goats I bought, yes, and paid for. I took them off your hands when you so foolishly ran away, but there was no thousand francs still due. Your troubles must have stolen your wits, Mère Mathilde. Move along if you please, there are other customers. And if you take groceries today, have the obligingness to pay for them."

Distressed to the point of hysteria, the old woman repeated in fuller detail the facts of the sale and the part payment. Friends wagged their heads in sympathy. Guichard stood unmoved.

"Have you a paper signed by me saying that I owe you a thousand francs? I always give a paper when I owe money. If you have not a signed paper the affair is closed. Next customer, please."

As the significance of the merchant's ultimatum sank into Mathilde's mind, she would have fallen had she not steadied herself against the counter. Her voice was agonized. "Oh, what can I say to make you remember? You must, you must! To deny it is robbery. You are telling a black lie and you know it."

"I forbid you to use such language in my store! Get on to your home," said Porky, his bald head red as a turkey's wattles. "Unless you have a paper you cannot collect a centime. You are beside yourself, old woman." His eyes were buttons of frozen ink.

Danielle, coming in at noon, found no fire, no meal, no soup. But in the bedroom, collapsed upon a chair, was a sobbing small figure in black.

Fully sharing Mathilde's indignation, the girl nevertheless felt that her first duty was to bolster the other's courage. "There must be a mistake," she soothed. "It's a blow, Grandmère, but we have had worse. We'll find a way out. There must be an eyewitness who saw him give us only a thousand francs."

She placed cold food upon the table, coaxed the grandmother to eat, and to swallow black coffee. Jeannot, aware of a family catastrophe beyond the comprehension of his seven years, was pale and quiet. The old dog by some subtle means felt the tension and tried to lick the girl's hand.

Danielle had a moment of faltering, when she was tempted to break down and weep too. If only she could talk to Pierre or Jeanne or Marc. But just thinking of them was a help, and she gulped back the weakness. "We've had much to contend with before, Grandmère, and we've always managed to find something to eat. Think how bad it was in Toulouse, and in Carcassonne. Let's not give that loathsome toad the satisfaction of thinking he can get us down. He can't. No one, nothing can stop us now. He thought we'd never come back. But he guessed wrong. From now on, I have two big targets in life: one is to bring our vineyard back, and the second is to get square with that crook." She poured more coffee for the old woman, and cuddled Jeannot beside her on the bench.

4. *Into Business*

TO THE rear of the Dufour stable, curtained by a
tangle of lustrous fig saplings, grew a cherry tree. Two
low-growing boughs formed a natural seat and arm rest.
Once one's head was leaning against the scratchy trunk
and one's feet were swinging clear of the ground, the world
and its alarms seemed a million miles away: one glimpsed
nothing but the darting swallows and the patches of blue
sky, and heard nothing but the restless leaves and the chirp
of insects.

The tree was Danielle's hide-out. Since childhood,
whenever she had felt the need of a good cry all by herself,
she had climbed to this seat. Here she had brought her
disappointments, and learned the hard lesson of becoming
reconciled to changes in her cherished plans. And here,
more than once, when she had been confronted by a blank
wall of opposition, she had discovered a little gate of escape
after thinking things through in the stillness.

On this day of the storekeeper's trickery, the girl's feet instinctively carried her to the cherry tree. She needed to be away from the sight of Mathilde's grief. She must take stock, logically and unhurriedly, of the family's changed circumstances. It was good to find her retreat again. During her absence the fig shoots had pushed higher; their lush, wide leaves gave more secure concealment. With her body relaxed against the trunk, her eyes lifted to the infinity above, her feet free of the earth, she sat absorbed a long time.

The completeness with which her grandmother had gone to pieces made it apparent that someone else must make the Dufour decisions. That could be no one but herself. Moreover, she must act quickly since only four hundred francs stood between them and actual debt. That very morning even Mathilde had been obliged to dip into their reserve. The plans for putting the vineyard in order, which she and Vivette had so gaily discussed yesterday, would have to be shelved. "My poor vines," she sighed, "once more you must be put aside."

She didn't know much about the law, but she conceded that Guichard had the facts when he boasted that, without a signed paper, they would never collect a centime from him. The credit at the store must be written off as non-existent. The alternative was plain. They must find work, at once, and for all of them. Work with wages paid every Saturday night.

Work didn't frighten her. During their wanderings she and Mathilde had washed dishes and scrubbed the floors of a hotel. She had cleaned cow stables, and Grandmère had made butter and cheese. They had weeded geranium fields for perfumers and gathered vegetables for market gardeners. Any job that came their way they had accepted gladly.

But in Arsac-le-Petit it was different, this hiring oneself out for wages. In their own village they had cultivated their land as proprietors, to feed themselves and their animals, to raise a crop to sell for their own account. There was dignity in that. It would be a distinct step down in the social scale to work on the land of others, take orders from them. The grandmother, who had been proud, would feel it. But beggars could not choose. They must eat. And without a struggle first, the Dufours would never borrow.

The girl straightened up. "It's got to be done. I'd better get at it. People will just be coming out from their siestas." But she did not leave her tree at once; she was still wishing she had some more-experienced adviser. Some man like Pierre or Ovide. Even Marc, for that matter. He wasn't much older, but his slow smile was so reassuring, so solid. Probably all he'd say would be, "Whatever you decide, Danielle, will be all right." But it would make all the difference in the world to have him where she could reach out and touch his arm.

It came in a flash. Why, of course, the best person to see was Monsieur le Curé. At that hour he would be in his garden, taking the air, in his canvas chair. For an instant she gratefully pressed her cheek against the bark; her cherry tree had not failed her.

In the thinly populated territory of Arsac-le-Petit, Father Ambrose occupied a privileged position. For fifty years he had been the shepherd of his parish. A halting speaker in the pulpit and prevented by asthma from physical exertion, he nevertheless enjoyed an influence without parallel in the department. It was due to plain, everyday, unassuming goodness of heart. One could not imagine Father Ambrose lending himself to an unkindness. High and low brought him their anxieties and by some mysterious inner sight he

was able to send them away with a solution. He might have
retired many years before; both his age and his infirmity
would have justified it. But he hung on—like a last leaf on
the tree, he would say, for his people's sake, knowing that
the bishop would not easily find a successor for so tiny a
parish.

From his reclining chair, by means of his grapevine
communication, the old man followed the details of his
parishioners' careers. His brain was like a card catalogue
of the past, the present, and the probable future of each of
them. Wise in the intricacies of the human heart, familiar
with family histories, he could predict what a man would
do, before he did it. He knew who were the reliable workers, who were the upright employers, what wage each was
worth, what each would be willing to pay. Monsieur le Curé
had married Danielle's parents and christened her; he was
a lifelong friend.

Fastened to the gate of the presbytery garden was a
circular spring, which in turn supported a bell. When the
gate stirred the spring trembled and the bell tinkled, announcing visitors to the priest and Sister Thermaline, his
elderly housekeeper.

Danielle was no sooner inside the sun-soaked enclosure
than she was recognized. Father Ambrose was just where
she had expected to find him. He closed his prayer book,
and held out both hands. His wrinkles creased in a smile
of welcome. The cheeks were rosy, like apples that are
shrunken, with the sweetness sealed within.

"My daughter, it is long since my eyes have had so glad a
sight. You are a big girl. In that you resemble your mother.
You are strong and good, that I can see for myself. But tell
me, have you news?"

Danielle's face sobered. Always the same question, always the same shake of the head. "No. I had hoped that it might be you who had heard something."

With quick sympathy the priest reached out and pressed her hand. "Patience, always patience. I never approach the altar without saying a prayer for Jeanne and Pierre and my other straying children. Faith tells me that somewhere they are longing for you, as you long for them. They are trying to come. What else can we do but have faith? For you and Mathilde patience is the highest form of courage."

Then Danielle told him of their sojourn with Mathilde's cousins, of their homesickness, of their journey north and west, of the unbearable silence enshrouding her parents. Lastly she told of the financial catastrophe of the morning, and the necessity of immediate work. "Four hundred francs, with prices as they are, will be gone before we can turn around," she concluded.

"I am not unprepared for what you relate of our storekeeper. Similar tales have come to me," said the priest. "But, let's get to the task at hand. What would be suitable for Mathilde, for Jeannot, and yourself? Our region is short of workers. You will have no difficulty if you are not too pressed. But we want the right thing, not to chop and change the second week."

He shaded his eyes with his hand. "The housekeeper at the Château tells me that the young ladies are inquiring for a woman experienced in fine laundering. They do not wish to consign their dainty garments to the common tub. Grandmère Dufour was once accomplished in that line. Would her strength be up to it still?"

"Of course it would," echoed the girl with enthusiasm. "It would be perfect for Grandmère. It is not heavy washing, only flimsy things. It would be no more than two or three days in the week. I will go there at once. May I say that you sent me?"

Father Ambrose was thinking aloud, slowly. "Mmmm. The Dumartins. The two boys have come home. Since their girl Arlette has married and left them they are without a woman to stir the lime-and-copper mixture and fill the sprayers when they treat their vines. They are obliged to employ a man, which is uneconomical. You know the work. You would sit on the cart, move the paddle in the barrel of solution, turn the faucet to fill the knapsacks. It would be for three days each week, perhaps four. And I may tell you in confidence that Papa Dumartin has sold his crop for a good price and can afford to pay well. He pays by the hour."

Danielle was on her feet. "I'd love that. As work it is nothing. Even before the war I used to serve the sprayers for my father and the Bracessacs. I'll go to the Dumartins the very first."

"As for the young Jeannot, it is not so simple," reflected the Curé. "He will be full of mischief—as he ought to be. He might water my vegetables, but to carry the two watering-pots would be too heavy. He might guard cows that pasture by the roadside. He would have to prevent them from being run down by automobiles, and keep them out of vines and crops. Blanche, the blacksmith's wife, has taken up dressmaking, and complains that watching her cows takes too much time. There are only the two, the cow and the heifer. She might give the boy a trial."

Father Ambrose turned a sidewise glance up to Danielle and she caught the good twinkle in his eye. "Well," she laughed, "Jeannot is only seven but old enough for mischief to be kept out of. And our dog Bergère is of the two the real expert with cows. In fact, *she* doesn't need a boy."

It was the priest's turn to laugh.

"Thank you, Father, thanks a thousand times," she said, eager to follow up his suggestions at once. "You always know the right thing. I was blue as indigo when I came. If these jobs don't turn out, may I come to see you again?"

"The more often, the more I shall be pleased, Danielle. And tell Mathilde to come. The asthma confines me to this chair, and so I welcome visitors."

Danielle thought of the dear old man sitting here, having to draw each breath with special care, in solitude and yet in touch with every soul in the valley. He might even know about Marc! Of course! If there was anything very hard to tell her, it was Father Ambrose who would have the moral strength and courage to do so. And she had expected poor little Vivette to tell her!

"Father," she began, "nobody seems willing to say anything to me about Marc. And I have not dared to go to see Agathe Bracessac, for fear there might be something about him too terrible—"

The Curé's face turned solemn but remained tender, and he shook his head, "No, my child, nothing more terrible than just no news at all." He seemed to understand at once almost everything that had been going on within her, as if she had been talking to him for hours, for he said: "We who remained behind in the village have got out of the habit of comment when there was no news. It only aired one's own anxiety to no other effect than exposing another's."

She nodded her comprehension: if she'd learned anything in the past harsh years it was the hundreds of small subtle things there were in which to be regardful of others' feelings. "Well," she said, straightening up and summoning all the spirit she could to leave the kind Curé with a grateful smile, "there's plenty to be done until we do hear from him, and I better get to it."

In the priest's look she saw that he thought of her feeling for Marc with a gravity that made it seem more serious and grownup than it had ever seemed before.

"Thank you, Father," she said quietly, and curtsied, bending her head forward, as she had done since she was in the first catechism class, while the old man laid his hand upon her head in blessing.

She was off with long strides. The gate bell tinkled. The priest reopened his book of prayers.

The grandmother was lighting the candle and cocked her head. A voice was singing. "If that's Danielle singing at a time like this, she has a cruel short memory." The old woman dabbed at her eyes. "Has she forgotten the misery that is upon us?"

As the girl dropped into a chair, still singing, her grandmother looked at her sharply. "You didn't tell me you were going out. I've been alone all the afternoon," the woman complained. "How can you look so happy when we are ruined? At least stop that singing."

"You'll sing too, my dear one," purred the girl, "when you hear my news. I'm sorry I left you, but I had business calls. I've walked seven or eight miles and feel fresh as a primrose. What you said yesterday about the people of Arsac being kind isn't half strong enough. Everywhere I went they treated me like an honored guest, not like a poor girl looking for work. It's all in the way you take them. If you smile they smile back. The people I've seen are nice enough to make up for that snake Guichard.

"Sit down, dear old worrier. Sit down and listen." Danielle was effervescent, the reaction after deep depression. "Each of us, you and Jeannot and myself, has a job. A job that is right for us, suitable to our strength. One that doesn't humiliate us."

Like magic Danielle's words wiped twenty years from the careworn face. As Mathilde listened one could imagine how she had looked as a young mother.

"First for yourself. The young ladies at the Château remember you and sent their regards. They remember the candied marrons you used to make for their Christmases. You are to wash their silk and drawn-work underthings. It will only mean a halfday at the washing-place, which won't tire your back. The chauffeur will bring the basket on Tuesday and come for it Saturday. And the pay will be high. They expect to pay what they pay in Paris."

With a cry that was part moan and part laughter, the grandmother covered her face with her open palms. "You are a clever girl, my Danielle," she said huskily. "Until you are old you will never know what this means to me. To be able to earn my way, in a work that is within my strength. And to have no charity in it. You do not know how fiercely the old cling to their independence."

Danielle caught her breath, humbled. There was something unearthly in the purity of joy that lit up the brave old features.

"And you will want to hear about Jeannot," the girl persisted gently. "I had to be very persuasive with Blanche. She thought he was not very serious, as of course he isn't. It was Bergère that decided her. Blanche will go with them for the first couple of days. If she puts a rope on old Pansy, the heifer will follow. Jeannot will not be paid money, but he will bring a quart of fresh milk home with him each night, and something from their garden for our supper. With no garden as yet I thought that would be useful. But whether he earns anything or not, it will be good to have him out of the way and feeling that he's doing something for his family."

"I for one think he's too young," Mathilde demurred. "But that will be Blanche's responsibility. But, little one, you haven't yet said what *you* are going to do."

"My job? It's a dream, truly! I work four days for Papa Dumartin, and have two full weekdays and Sunday for our own vines. I'm to tend the sulphate barrel for him. And, Mathilde, I'm to be paid *eight francs an hour!* My dear, we are going to roll in money."

The Grandmère hugged herself and rocked with joy. "Ah! To have been so low at noon and brought up so high by evening, it—it sharpens the appetite." She pushed the preparation for supper. To her surprise two of her pullets had laid, and she was going to fête the occasion by making a potato-and-onion omelette. As she worked she related anecdotes of their new employers, the Château family and the Dumartins.

Danielle welcomed the interruption. It seemed that since her return to Arsac, her tongue had loosened up greatly. There was so much to ask and to tell, so much business to negotiate. Her whole face was tired from having done so much talking.

They sat long over their meal, the good old Arsac-le-Petit custom. Their first day at home had been certainly a crowded one.

"I'll make faggots while the wood is soft," Mathilde murmured to herself, while Danielle sat silent, trying to frame her words for her next remark. Now was the time to tell her grandmother of still another transaction, one that she'd been almost afraid to confess: it had been so daring a one.

"There is something more, Grandmère, something you may not like. I did it on impulse, but I feel it was good sense. If our Jeanne and Pierre were here now and knew the fix that Porky has put us in, I'm sure they'd approve of what I did."

The grandmother sat up apprehensively and clasped her hands under her chin. Danielle felt she must break it even more gradually to her.

"You see, dear, what we liked about the credit at the store was that it gave us a sense of security, kept worry from our minds while we got back on our feet. It was like having a sack full of potatoes and a salted pig in a barrel. Now, your washing for the Château and my working for Dumartin will pay for our day-to-day needs, food. But what about an emergency, like needing a doctor, or paying taxes? When I was making my visits this afternoon, that thought came to me again and again, and it really frightened me. Then, I realized that the biggest thing Porky stole from us was the feeling that we need not be afraid. I saw then that that was more valuable to me, at least, than money or property. If I'd been a little more scared I might have lost the nerve to go out looking for work."

"Yes, that's so. My grandmother used to say the snake is jealous of the bird's wings, and so he paralyzes her with fear first so she can't fly away. Then he eats her."

"Exactly, Grandmère dear. Well, there was the auto of the

sawmill contractor standing in front of Gustav Bernalou's. I had a hunch it would be a good thing for me to wait and speak to him. I was as cool as lettuce. I told him that we had some first-growth pines in our lot that needed to be thinned out, and reminded him that the price of timber was so high it might be a good time for him to pick up some. He looked interested, so I put it right to him: how much would he give me for ten trees? He answered one hundred twenty-five francs a tree. I said I wanted a hundred-fifty. Then he looked at me queerly and said he'd give a hundred-forty-five. All right, I told him, but leave us the tops and branches for firewood."

The grandmother unclasped her tense hands and brought them together again excitedly as if in applause.

"Someone might say that selling those trees reduces the value of our property," Danielle plunged ahead, "but I think, on the contrary, that it increases it. Well, he had a pruning-bill in his car, and we drove over and marked the ten. And there and then he paid me and *here* is the money! To be put under your mattress and forgotten." She smoothed the bills upon the table, placing a plate over them. "We'll carry on with our washing and vine-spraying, and live on what we earn. But inside ourselves we will know that we aren't afraid of tomorrow."

The old woman's hands had come unclasped again and were held in amazement over the windfall. "That makes twice today you've done well, my Danielle." Then she settled back reflectively and said, "My Jules planted those pines from seed, just after we were married. He said they'd be a help in our old days. Ah, it's an old truth; people who plant trees never can tell whom they'll benefit, but they'll always benefit someone."

Danielle was beginning to feel the need of rest after so active a day. She yawned: "If I'm to be on top of Papa Dumartin's oxcart at seven-thirty I'd better get myself to bed."

She was half undressed, sitting on the edge of the bed, when the thought came to her, where were Jeanne and Pierre and Marc laying their heads tonight? Certainly on no bed like this. And what were they planning for the morrow? What new homeward effort? Oh, if she could but get the least hint of news!

5. *The Dowry Field*

OVER a week passed, with days full of hard work but no news.

The first bell for nine o'clock Mass was ringing. Mathilde called from the kitchen, "Hurry or we'll be late. Your dress is on the bed."

Danielle, hammer in hand and her mouth full of nails, was mending the gate to the chicken run. "Coming," she stuttered through the nails.

The old lady had spent a high-pressure week with needle,

thread, and shears, upon the contents of the cupboard and chest that filled the wall space of her bedroom. More than one tear had fallen upon Pierre's black suit and Jeanne's dresses as she shook out the creases and spread them upon the hedge to air.

Upon their first Sunday at home they had had nothing wearable. Everything of Danielle's was outgrown by several sizes. They had walked to and from Mass in their travel-grimed clothes. But it would not occur twice, Mathilde had vowed with a snap in her eye. Therefore, each afternoon she had ripped, stitched and suffered professional advice, under the live oak in Marisma's courtyard. For herself she was sponging and turning her black serge. For Danielle she was remodeling Jeanne's blue wool dress. The arms and shoulders would need no change, although the waist was too full and the skirt too long. Mathilde felt no little

satisfaction as she finally hung the blue dress on its hanger that Saturday night.

The second bell tolled ominously.

Danielle rushed in, splattered water to left and right, dove into her clothes. The grandmother was assembling a picnic lunch, for they had planned, after Mass, to change back into work clothes and spend the balance of the day at the Dowry Field.

"I have potato salad, hard eggs, little onions and sandwiches. Do you think that will be enough? Jeannot will have his cows along the Avensan road, so that we can eat together. I have a bottle of milk for him and piquette for us. To save time after Mass I might as well bring the sickle and grubhoe from the shed now."

The field in question lay a quarter-mile outside the village. But as nothing had been planted upon it since Pierre's mobilization, and as the women had been occupied in the opposite direction, they had not visited it since their return.

Danielle, dressed for Mass, stood framed in the doorway; tall and flat, with wide shoulders. Glossy braids were coiled close to her head in a crown. Her mouth was generous, her eyes widely spaced, her nose finely chiselled. Her teeth showed whiter against the weather-bronzed skin. She was wearing her mother's black shoes and stockings and a small felt hat from the chest. Not pretty, as Vivette was pretty, her face was a blending of strength and sweetness. She was clean, brisk, wholesome, just stepping from girlhood into womanhood. Her hands, supple and competent, neither art nor nature could have improved.

The grandmother uttered a cry of pleasure. "My dear ... you look ... you look ... not just anybody ... you look like someone distinguished ... the kind that people turn ...

and look at twice. Blanche did well to insist upon the lawn bands at the neck and cuffs."

"And it's you I have to thank for it, old mother hen." The girl was blushing a little under her tan, as she bent and kissed Mathilde on the forehead.

"But, march, march. You know how Father Ambrose, once he has started, detests the noise of people entering."

The priest's asthma was troublesome, which abbreviated the sermon. By eleven o'clock, the nearly new-looking wardrobe having been displayed among Mathilde's peers, she and her granddaughter changed for the uniforms of agriculture. They locked the door, deposited the key under its brick, shouldered their tools and lunch, and were off to the Dowry Field, the most coveted eight acres in the commune of Arsac-le-Petit.

In the southwest of France is a tract of marsh and scrub forest known as the Landes of Gascony. It is a peculiar geological formation dating from the Ice Age. At that period, under immense overhead pressure, vegetable fiber was impregnated with sand and clay. A sheathing of waterproof hardpan, like a thin layer of cement and locally known as "alios," was formed, a foot or two beneath the surface of the ground. Because of the alios, the rainwater is prevented from seeping through the subsoil. Stagnant bogs, a desolation of heather and swordgrass, stretch to the horizon. Wild pigs root in the muck. Foxes stalk the heron and the plover. Shepherds in shaggy coats, high on stilts and served by white-eyed Labrit dogs, graze their sheep. Mule teams, without bit or bridle, whose business it is to haul resin, charcoal and mine props toward civilization, plunge into the maze of overgrown wheeltracks and vanish from sight. And smothering everything, unescapable as the weather, toss the plumes of gorse and broom, evergreen in winter burnished gold in spring.

Arsac-le-Petit could be called a frontier town. For as a seaside village lies upon the shore of the sea, Arsac lies upon the fringes of the Landes. A short mile to the east of Ste. Philomène's spire the undrained marshes begin.

The Dowry Field was alios, but some far-off Dufour ancestor had reclaimed it. With maul and pickaxe he had smashed through the hardpan, and dug ditches to drain the sour water into the Lorina brook. As his reward he became the owner of a quadrangle of warm light humus, which could be relied upon to produce harvests of beans, oats, corn, and potatoes. It had been hand-cultivated for so many seasons, enriched by so many oxcarts of barnyard manure, that it was crumbly, black, and a pleasure to till.

The name, Dowry Field, stemmed from a family tradition. The Field went to the eldest daughter of each generation as her marriage dot. Mathilde had it from her mother, and since she herself had no daughter, it went to her son's wife, Jeanne, when the latter joined the family. In due course it would come to Danielle when she married. In a region where fortunes were small, and where land and what grows upon it were the most esteemed form of wealth, the eventual possession of the Dowry Field established Danielle socially, as a substantial person of the community.

On their way to the Field, the grandmother and the girl came upon Jeannot and his charges.

"Come, Jeannot, speed up your old cow," cried Matilde with pretended ill-temper. "The day is half gone. We needn't expect to accomplish much today. If we can cut back the blackberry canes and grub out the thistles before they go to seed, it will be something. I hate to think how the field will look after lying idle for three seasons. My Jules babied it like a child. Yet they do say that it enriches land to lie fallow." The old lady rambled on amiably, and Jeannot tugged at Pansy, the cow.

A hush descended upon the trio, a hush that was speechlessness. They were opposite the Dowry Field. Open-mouthed, the women stared at the field and at one another.

"You've got the wrong place," piped the boy. "This can't be the right road."

"But it is! Of course it is," insisted Danielle in a strangled voice. "There is the tree in the center, the willows along the stream, the pine woods on all three sides. Of course it's our field."

But instead of being a jungle of weeds, the land was beautifully clean, planted in neat rows. Corn stood shoulder high. The potatoes were hilled. Bean pods were plump. It was skillful farming, done by an expert.

"I don't like this," exclaimed Mathilde angrily. "If someone is having games with us, someone is going to get hurt. Eat your lunch, my children, and we'll come back to find out how this has come about."

"Don't you think someone did it for a present? They wanted to surprise us?" Jeannot wondered.

Mathilde frowned. "No I don't, I'm sorry to say. We have friends, but no friends who would go to all this trouble. It was a man working strictly for himself who cultivated these crops. But how, in the names of the saints, did he get hold of our field?"

Danielle was remembering things. "Do you know, I was half expecting something strange. I didn't know what it would be, but many little things set me wondering. Now they add up. The first morning, in the shop, Victor and Blanche gave each other a mysterious look, but she shook her head. The Curé almost said something, but stopped sharp. It looks as though people had a conspiracy to keep us in the dark about something."

"Now that you mention it," Mathilde confirmed, "I've had suspicions. At Marisma's, while we were sewing, there have been awkward pauses, when I knew they were saying one thing but thinking another. Old Thérèse Bernalou came from Ligondra and started to tell me she was so sorry, but Marisma jumped like she had a hot coal in her ear, and led Thérèse away. Well, if Victor knows the meaning of our Field being planted he's going to have a chance to tell the whole story, chapter and verse. Goodbye, Jeannot. Eat my lunch, too; I'd choke if I tried to swallow. Be home at the regular time, when the sun gets down to the roof of Odette's barn." She and Danielle hurried back to the village.

Seated in the blacksmith's kitchen, Mathilde did not waste a second. "Victor, we want the story of our Field. Who planted it? How did they come to do it? Out with it all."

The man fidgeted, exchanged glances with his wife. Of the two she was the more composed.

"Yes, tell them," said Blanche. "They'll have to know the dirty business sometime."

"Lawyer Blanchard did it according to law. We couldn't stop him," Victor began.

"That isn't the beginning. What was the very first thing?" commanded the intent old woman.

"The underlying motive was that Porky Guichard had wanted your Field for years. So have others. But Porky didn't care how he got it. He has made a good deal of money selling supplies to the occupation troops, and he saw a trick that he could put through. I was away myself. Most Arsac men were with the army, There was no one to speak up for Pierre. Lawyer Blanchard and Porky have no more human decency than a frozen turnip."

Blanche fetched the coffeepot from the fireplace and poured each a cup. Victor lighted up his pipe. "It's going to take some time and we might as well be comfortable." Mathilde did not move her eyes from the blacksmith's face by as much as a hair's breadth.

"The months passed, nothing being heard of Pierre and Jeanne. Rumor said that he was in a prison hospital, badly wounded. You know what kind of medical treatment people get in a place like that. Rumor said that the factory where Jeanne worked had been bombed and a falling girder had broken her back. Mind you, these were no more than rumors. Porky may have invented them himself. He's in a good position, there in the store, to originate false reports. You and the children had been swallowed up in the ocean of wanderers.

"That was the situation when Guichard turned up in Blanchard's office with a bill as long as your arm. He claimed that it covered Pierre's purchases of supplies over a period of four years. Anyone who knew Pierre would have repudiated that bill; Pierre was prompt and careful. But Porky had the accounts all in order, the dates, the items, and the prices. And there wasn't a soul who could contradict him. He said he had waited long enough and he needed his money.

"Blanchard did things in a strictly legal way. He nailed a writ on the town clerk's door for thirty days. He inserted a warning in the Bordeaux papers informing Pierre Dufour or his next of kin that a parcel of land belonging to said Dufour was to be sold at public auction to satisfy a debt. When the sale came off, Guichard bought the land. Then he farmed it out to Roger l'Eglise, over in Pice village. What you have seen today are Roger's crops.

"The field was sold for six thousand francs more than Porky's alleged bill. That surplus is in Blanchard's office, waiting for any of the Dufour family to claim it." It was hurting Victor to tell these deplorable facts, but he kept on doggedly.

"There were wartime regulations for the protection of soldiers which might have delayed the sale, had anyone invoked them in Pierre's favor. But there was no one. Blanchard excused himself by saying that it was an ordinary commercial debt and, as the merchant insisted upon having his money, he, as a lawyer, could only proceed as the law provided. There, Grandmère Mathilde, is the story of the Dowry Field."

"But there must be some way for us to get it back." The old lady brought her fist down upon the table. "There used to be justice for poor people in France. We don't have to sit like dead mice and be robbed."

"Yes," said the blacksmith, "there is a way. It will be long and costly, but there is a way. First, you must pay Guichard's original bill with interest. Next you must reimburse the costs of the sale, which included Blanchard's fees. Lastly you must pay the estimated value of l'Eglise's work on the land and the value of his crops. It would amount to a ruinous sum, and, as you would have three clever men against you, they might drag it out for years. You would need to borrow the money for all this, and, in addition, the money to pay lawyers to fight Blanchard."

Mathilde's courage drained away as Victor was recounting the almost insurmountable obstacles to regaining her field.

She was just a shriveled-up old woman, with the pitiful eyes of a trapped animal, when he concluded.

"But that's not the line I would want to take," said the man gently. "You must realize that Blanche and I have talked this over many evenings until midnight. We thought that if you returned, you would come to us for advice. And here is the advice that I would give my own mother.

"Let us be reasonable. You are no longer young. You have two children to bring up. One of them is a pretty masterful child"—he smiled at Danielle—"but she is still a minor. Why not let the matter of the Dowry Field drop, as one more of the war's casualties? You have your house and garden, the wood land and the vines, plenty for you all. Take the six thousand francs the lawyer has for you, buy some goats and a couple of cows, as you used to have, and go back to making cheeses. You were famous for that. Do this, rather than saddle yourself with a lawsuit that will beggar you and may destroy your peace of mind for the rest of your years. It may look like a tame surrender, but I am convinced that it is the part of wisdom. Ask any fair-minded friend and I think that he will advise you the same."

"Never, Victor, never!" Up to this point Danielle had said nothing. Now her fingers clutched the edge of the table and her eyes were dark with anger. "What you say may be all right for Grandmère, but it doesn't suit me. Besides, the field concerns her indirectly. She has had her use of it, she and her children. Jeanne has had her use of it. The future of the Field is for me and my children."

She walked to the door to look out, and turned back saying, "What you say is good advice for old people. They haven't much time, they can't wait. But I can wait. This noon, that field, level and clean, was beautiful. There was enough on it to feed two families, five families. It should be mine, mine and my children's. You say that we have three venge- ful men against us. I don't care if there are ten. I'll not stop fighting to keep what's mine until I stop breathing."

"Good for you," Blanche cried. "That's what I like to hear."

"What's more, I think I can prove that my father never owed Guichard, or anybody else that much money or any money that long. I know for sure that he didn't. The last afternoon before he was mobilized he sold his crop to the manager of Château Cantenac and collected the money. When he got home he handed a roll of bills to my mother, saying, 'Make it last as long as you can. But you can rest easy in your mind; I've been around and paid everybody. We don't owe a centime.' That night he took the train."

Mathilde came in, "There! There! That's right. I remem- ber that too."

"If my father did not owe Guichard money, then Guich- ard is a criminal, from first to last. We know he's a liar about Mathilde's cow and goats. It makes me wild to have that odious cheat saying that my father walked out on his bills. Pierre has been an honest man all his life. If he is dead, he died for France. He was not like that pig who skulked be- hind his counter thinking up robberies. It's not Christian, but I'd like to see Porky chopped into little pieces and fried in oil."

"*Bien, bien, ma petite!*" Victor was rubbing his hands. "It lifts my soul to hear words like that from the young. My girl, if you do not weaken in your spirit, and will have patience, there will be fifty men in this village who will sustain you."

Mathilde's courage had revived. She was sitting erect,

nodding in agreement, doubtfully at first, but at the end with full conviction. The girl was impatient to follow up her advantage.

"Here's what we'll do, Grandmère. It is Sunday afternoon and Maître Blanchard will be in his summer house. We will take a receipt from him that he holds six thousand francs for Pierre Dufour or his heirs. That paper we will guard preciously. But we will also tell him firmly that, for us, the matter of the Dowry Field is not closed. We do not relinquish our right to re-open the case. If we do not accept the money it will show that we do not accept that the case is ended. Come along, Grandmère." The old woman was already standing. A stronger will had asserted itself and she was pathetically ready to follow it.

"Thank you, Victor, and thank you, Blanche, for the coffee. We needed it, but we feel better now," said Danielle. "If you don't mind, we'll leave our tools and pick them up on the way home."

The stars were out. A blurred figure was stumbling toward the cherry tree. As she had sat after supper, a devastating thought had come to Danielle, and she must be alone.

"That's why Vivette wouldn't talk about Marc. That's why I haven't been able to shake anything out of her. She knew about the Field, and she didn't want me to count on Marc. She judged him just as anyone else would. He's only human. Even Father, that day when he said to Ovide that we'd make a nice couple, said that I'd have the Dowry

Field, as though that were terribly important. When I had the Field I was somebody, any of the boys would marry me. Without the Field I'm just another poor girl, not even pretty, working for wages, living with her grandmother. Vivette is sure Marc won't have me now, and she's trying to get my mind off him."

Her arms hugged the trunk of the tree. "Oh, oh, my Marco, they have stolen you from me too . . ."

Around her were the sleepy sounds of the summer night. But all she heard was the bereaved cry of her own heart.

6. *In Her Neighbor's Vineyard*

ON TOP of Papa Dumartin's oxcart, Danielle found the oxen, in their fly-blankets, dull company, never budging except to flick an ear or bring up a cud. There were five men: Papa Dumartin, his two sons Abel and René, and two neighbors. Like Danielle, the neighbors were hired by the day.

She would watch the men, each with a sprayer on his back, like a knapsack, walking the rows between the vines and spraying them with lime-and-bluestone mixture to fight off blight and mildew. As the men tramped up and down the rows, each became the nucleus of a small cloud of vapor, robin's-egg blue. The mist dried on their faces, hands, and clothing, and after but an hour's work they looked like a procession of statues made of tinted chalk. It was hard work, the incessant pull of a forty-five pound knapsack on a man's shoulders while with one hand he worked the handle of the pressure pump and with the other directed the nozzle so as to saturate both the underside and the top side of each leaf, little or big.

Every so often a man would emerge with an empty knapsack from the leafy alley he'd been working, back up to the high cart, and grunt. Danielle would pull the plug from his knapsack, turn the faucet of the barrel of mixture, and listen. As a milky blue stream flowed into the reservoir bag, the escaping air would whistle in a rising scale, so she could tell by ear when the bag was filled. Then at the right moment she'd shut off the faucet and replace the cork. The man would give another grunt and plod toward his next row. Boss or helper, it was the same unrelieved strain upon the shoulders, no rest from it even while he backed up against her cart awaiting a refill.

It bothered her that men could be so regardless of their own small working comforts. So one evening she rummaged in the loose lumber of the Dufour barn until she found a timber end, a block about a foot long and six inches thick. She ran a piece of wire through a knothole, and next morning, after the men had had their first fill, she wired the block to the floor-edge of the cart.

Abel Dumartin was the first man to return for a fill-up. He was as much a grunter as any of the others.

"Give your shoulders a little toss," she told him, "so the bottom of your sprayer will rest on this block."

Abel, a dour, grumpy young man, looked down at the block questioningly but did as he was told. Although he said nothing as the filling went on, she could see the crease on his cheek, which meant he was grinning. Men! Afraid to spoil young girls with too much praise!

But she was glad she had thought to do this. She could let herself half imagine that one of these men might be

Marc—wherever he might be now—receiving easement from her bit of ingenuity. It worked so well! As the morning advanced, she noticed how the men gratefully ran their fingers under the loosened straps, to soothe the pinched muscles. They pulled their sticky shirts from the skin for a moment's ventilation. Every time they came to the cart it meant a fifty-second respite from the weight. To lengthen the rest, as the sun mounted higher, she contrived not to open the faucet all the way.

Not even Papa Dumartin suspected her little trick. He wore a disreputable straw hat, high in the peak, drawn down to protect his eyes. It made him resemble a stubby bird, with crest, peak, and side-paddle wings. "You look for all the world like a big blue bird," Danielle laughed, "Papa Bluebird!" The old man scratched his blue nose with his blue thumb. It was a novelty to have this playful talk. He'd been missing it since his own jolly daughter Arlette had married and moved away. After that, when he came for a refill, he chirped and flapped his arms, playing up to her.

"I'm cheating, Papa," she said, "I have the faucet running just a bit slower to give you birds a little more rest while the sun is hottest."

"Ssh!" he said, winking, "don't tell the boss!"

No one mentioned the back-rest to her, but when she was eating her lunch on the bench outside the Dumartin kitchen, she overheard the tag-end of something Papa was relating to his wife. "That girl of Pierre's is no fool, and so light-hearted, makes you feel younger just having her around."

"Light-hearted, indeed," she thought, "after that scoundrel Guichard has cheated Marc and me of our Dowry Field. And every minute in the day an ache inside of me longing to see him and my parents home and well."

The men all referred to her as "that girl of Pierre's" and this pleased her. It showed, indirectly, that they still considered Pierre alive. It related her with one they esteemed. And the day would come when she would call upon that esteem to redeem his honor in the village and to get the Dowry Field restored to her rightful possession. There wasn't much she could do besides be patient until her chance came to strike back at Guichard and Blanchard, but meanwhile her natural inclination toward deepening her friendship with people wouldn't be a waste of time either.

One of the hired men, for instance, who wore no stockings inside his sabots, had got a blister on his heel where the wooden edge rubbed it. Danielle noticed his limp. "Look here, Batiste," she whispered, "I'll get some butter for that heel." And she did, by the time he returned for his next fill-up. To save him the embarrassment of being overseen by the others while a young girl fussed over him, she took him around the opposite side of the cart, where she made him a bandage of clean cloth. Batiste thanked her with a slow smile. He was about thirty-five and had so large a flock of children at home, that he rarely got any fussing-over himself.

She told herself that while learning viniculture she was also learning something about menfolk: that they fall into working-habits which dulled them to any sense about their own comfort and the improved efficiency they'd get from it. Also, that they liked to be fussed over, almost like little boys, treated like Jeannot. Maybe because they needed it? "Oh, my Marc, where are you?..."

Batiste returned for another fill-up. "It works fine, Danielle," he said pointing to his foot. "I'm your friend for life. Anytime I can do you a good turn just say so."

There atop the cart she sat thinking, thinking in between fill-ups. She brought her comb each morning and gave her hair a thorough going over. She polished her nails, a thing she'd never had time for before, using a stroking trick Vivette had shown her during one of the rare hours they now had to see each other. Since the treachery of the Dowry Field, Danielle had several times mentioned Marc to her, and each time Vivette would shake her head sadly or give Danielle a gentle hug, as if to say, what good can any words of mine do?

Papa Dumartin came up for a fill. "Well, Danielle, how do you like this job by now? You look so—so over-serious up there."

"I don't like it, Papa, because there's not enough of it. I'm idle two-thirds of the time. You pay me eight francs each hour for twenty minutes' work, and you and I are both losers. I sit up here and think of my troubles."

"Ah, my dear little friend," he mumbled in his deep-toned voice, "I understand. Something, maybe, to put your mind on your hands eh, instead of on itself?"

At his next trip to the barrel Papa had an idea. "Mama has rheumatism in her hands. She makes heavy weather with the darning, and three men walk the heels out of a lot of socks."

"Perfect," cried Danielle. "I'm no champion darner, but Mama can give me a lesson or two, if she likes."

And Mama Dumartin certainly did. She was enchanted, having a woman near her again on the big, many-manned farm. "Never mind what color yarn you use," she said, examining Danielle's first effort. "All colors wear alike."

The old couple had missed having their daughter around the house. Arlette rode over an afternoon or two a week on her bicycle, but it was not the same thing any more. It was visiting, helping a bit perhaps with the chores, discussing family matters. But it wasn't having her working-day life engaged with theirs, as it was with that girl of Pierre's.

Soon it became Danielle's habit, once the last fill-up of the morning was made, to skip over to the house, set the table, rinse and season the salad, and line the earthen soup bowls with thin slices of bread, while the men fed the animals, and washed up.

After the meal, while the menfolk dozed and smoked, she wiped the dishes and arranged them in the cupboard. Mama preferred to wash because the hot water took the swelling out of her hands. This division of labor gave Danielle a hot meal at noon, without the walk home, and she knew that she earned it.

And all the time, at the back of her head, plans were unfolding—plans for their land, for Mathilde, for Jeannot, and herself. They were paying their way, without dipping into the reserve under Mathilde's mattress. Danielle even had a pair of new shoes. Their vines were healthier, they had been plowed and weeded, and a two-day rain had freshened the color. By another autumn they should give a luscious account of themselves. Danielle worked on them two days a week and on Sunday afternoon. For the coming spring she would need wire, acacia pickets, lime, sulphur, and copperas. Above all, their vines needed a thorough and expert pruning, such as only an experienced vineyardman could give.

Her plans embraced the future as well. Suppose Pierre should not return. Nor Marc. The responsibility would be all hers. Beside the lamented Dowry Field and their vines, the Dufours owned three parcels of land, gravel land that was prime for grapes, but unprofitable for tillage. These three plots should be planted and bearing fruit by the time Jeannot was old enough to work them.

But she, as a girl, knew a mere smattering of the fine points of the culture and the making of wine. She could hoe out the weeds and lop off the tendrils, that was about all. The old people called the vine a jealous mistress, for you must be doing something for it all the time. But she didn't know just what. Some years they required two sprayings, other years, nine or ten. She would not know how to detect the fatal mushrooms at the joints. Nor how to prevent the juice from becoming vinegar. This was men's work, specialists' work. Pierre had not thought it necessary to teach her.

Here she was—on the ox-cart and in the Dumartin house—in a veritable schoolroom, if she were not too stupid to learn. The man for whom she was working had the lore at his finger tips and was good-humored about answering questions. The Dumartins' wine was rated as Gentlemen's Wine by the brokers and buyers. It was aged without haste, a brilliant ruby in color, round and bland in flavor. And it had the distinction of being sold, not under the town name, but under the name of their own property.

If she was ignorant she could learn. And she did. She asked why some of the vines had yellow leaves and what to do about it. She asked why, on some vines, the grapes were dropping from the stems. She asked why some farmers were painting the roots with whitewash, why others were splashing arsenic over the leaves. She asked whether there was something she could do to combat the robber bands of wasps that were sucking the juice. And how did Papa Dumartin tell which of the sections of the vineyard should be sprayed next?

She stood at the old man's elbow when he sniffed into

dry barrels and sniffed right after him, to see if there were a smell of mustiness. She remained after hours while he made fresh spraying mixture for the following morning. At length he allowed her to weigh the lime and bluestone and compound the mixture herself. And as she sat on the cart she wrote in a notebook about symptoms of the vine sicknesses, functions of the different ingredients, and signs of perfect health in plants.

She had not been working long for the Dumartins before she was struck by a certain peculiarity of theirs. Every other family that she knew was complaining about the shortage of supplies, the impossibility of finding quicklime, sulphur, wire, sulphate of copper. But Papa never grumbled. Even the wholesale dealers in Bordeaux did not stock the chemicals that were necessary to produce a crop. But by some sleight-of-hand the right things, in the right quantity, always turned up in the Dumartin storeroom at the right time. The girl was sure that the old man enjoyed some secret, inside short cut to the source of supply.

About this matter, though, it would be impertinent, she felt, to ask questions. But another season she would need these materials. All she could do now was to keep her ears open.

Arlette's husband, André, was an enterprising young vineyardman of Castelnau. They had bicycled over for the afternoon and were just saying goodbye when Danielle overheard Papa Dumartin remark to his son-in-law, "You won't forget to include fifty kilos of sulphate for me in your next order."

"No. I'll put it with mine when the Co-operative sends in its requisition next week."

So that was it? A thing in Castelnau called a "co-operative." And André appeared to know all about it. In her notebook she jotted: "André—Co-operative—Castlenau," and strode homeward.

That *must* be it, the Dumartin secret! If it wasn't a secret, then why hadn't they told others about it? But still, they must have known she was within earshot, when they blurted out that word co-operative. And they knew her by now, with her ears greedy to pick up anything. Goodness, she had to! If she was going to make out with the farm she'd have to find out about *everything* before another spring.

Co-operative. It sounded vague. In the cities she'd seen such names on some of the business houses. The word itself meant working together, she could see that. But *who* working together? And behind the scenes, it seemed. Like Porky Guichard and the lawyer Blanchard? Oh, if Papa Dumartin should be engaged in anything like that, she'd no longer believe that honesty was a real thing in the world but only something to dangle in front of simple-minded people to make them all the easier to cheat. The thought made the evening darkness come down heavily upon her spirit.

7. *Strangers in the Dusk*

SOME distance ahead of her on the road, she saw a tall figure walking stumblingly. Somebody, she guessed, who had been drinking too much. Ordinarily, she wouldn't have felt afraid, she knew; but just now, in the half-light of what had ended as a dubious day, and along this particular lonely piece of road, she dreaded encountering a stranger.

For a while she slowed up, then decided this wouldn't do. The man might look back and think she was following him. Better take her regular stride and pass him on the far side of the road. After all, she had to remember that she could take care of herself. If he should speak to her she would answer his question, bid him a good evening kindly (for let no traveler have cause to speak ill of the courtesy of Arsac), and then be on her way.

Through the dusk, as she neared him, she made out a musette bag bumping on his left side and slung from his other shoulder. He swung his left arm out to clear the bag, but he did not swing his free arm at all. There was something wrong with it, the way it hung straight down, idle at his side. Crippled—poor fellow! She knew what it felt like to be a stranger on a lonely road at this forlorn hour of the day. As she got nearer still she saw he was gaunt as a scarecrow, in soldier clothes.

He must have heard her, for he turned a little to glance back at her, then wearily pulled his head forward as he trudged on. He had a bearded face. Suddenly he turned again, all the way around, and faced her. His jaw fell open and his eyes blinked, widening under the matted fringe of uncut hair hanging over them.

"Are you—? Yes," he said.

Everything stopped dead in her for a moment until a familiar sound in the aftertone of his voice awoke her from her benumbed stare from the opposite side of the road.

"You can't recognize me?" he was saying harshly, with a hurt laugh. "My name is—"

"O-oh, Marc—!" she cried out, her voice breaking with the feeling within her. She made to spring toward him, then checked herself, held back every emotion lest she break down completely and make it all the more difficult.

"You needn't apologize," he was saying as she came nearer, a half-kindly, half-bitter note in his tone, "I know how I look."

"You look, you look much taller," she countered, trying to make herself understand that this skeleton thing was what her Marc could have become in the war. "You must be at least a half head taller."

"You—you look taller too," he said, but made no move to approach her. It was as if she seemed as strange to him as he to her. She wanted to offer to relieve him of the musette bag, and decided not to: she had to be careful, knowing how resentful a disabled soldier could be at any suspicion of pity.

She reached her hands to him, though, and after a moment's hesitation, he raised his left hand a little, took hers for a brief timid grasp, and let go.

"To think of meeting you first thing," he muttered, looking away, and then gave her a side glance. "Why are you walking on this road this time of the day, I wonder?"

"I'm coming from Dumartin's."

"Oh? How's René?" He toed at a pebble in the road. "Pretty big, by now?"

"I'm working there, in the vineyard."

"Working?"

"Yes, Marc," she said, taking his hand, and starting to walk homeward. "As you must have noticed everywhere, a lot of people have become poor, and the women have to pitch in and make up for the missing menfolk."

"Same story everywhere," he agreed, not taking his hand away and yet not grasping hers. His hand was feverishly warm, but with its indifference to her it seemed distant, as he himself did, more distant, in a way, than he ever seemed during their long separation. "How's my grandmother?" he asked dully, but as if he were hardening himself to hear bad news. "Is she still living?"

"Very much so. Anxious about you, no word in all this time."

He let go of her hand, pulled in a breath, and clenched his teeth tight.

The stars were appearing in the great dismal sky, and they seemed like something truly familiar in comparison to this changed Marc at her side.

"But you didn't hear from us either," she said. "Grandmère, Jeannot, and I took out before the enemy got here, and we didn't get back for nearly three years."

He still kept his teeth clenched.

"Pierre and Jeanne are still missing. As it was with you, we still don't know if they are alive or dead."

At last he said in a low, husky voice, "So you had it hard too?"

"We had our share of it."

The lights of the village windows appeared just ahead of them, and he stopped to contemplate them.

"Listen to me and understand this, here and now," he said without looking at her but down into Arsac. "I've held out deliberately for more than two months against coming back here, like this. And now that I'm doing it, I want you to know, I don't expect anything. You don't owe me anything."

She seized his hand again, but he pulled it away.

"You understand me?"

"Yes." The same old strong-willed, independent Marc, but what a stranger these old traits made of him!

He looked at her probingly a moment and dropped his gaze.

"Come, let's go down by the short cut to your house," she said. They passed through a gap in the hedge.

She saw he was almost too weak to move. That hand of his felt feverishly hot. He was a sick man, and yet she dared not offer him the least support.

As they approached Agathe's cottage, he became more nervous.

"Will you let me go ahead a bit and prepare your grandmother, Marc? I think I can make it easier for both of you."

He nodded passively and she left him on the bench under the fig tree, where his grandfather and his father had sat through many a long meditation. But he flopped down on it as though it were any bench.

Judging by the lantern light, Danielle figured the old woman was in the milking shed, and there she was, stripping the third goat.

"Listen, Grandmère," she began. "I have good news, wonderful news."

The old woman turned with a trustful, enquiring smile.

"But it's not *all* good."

The submissive, waiting smile did not change.

"Marc is back."

Agathe threw up her arms. "Where, where is he?"

"He's not well. He has a—a bad arm, and a fever. We'll have to handle him carefully."

"How do you mean?" The old woman was trembling all over, and kept nodding her head eagerly as Danielle told her he was perhaps on the edge of a breakdown, looked starved and that one mustn't get upset at anything he said. "I know, I know, dearie, I've had soldiers come back from wars before." She picked up the lantern. "Please, bring the milk, little sweetheart! I'm afraid I'll break into a run."

She trotted out toward the house, and Danielle waited a moment before picking up the bucket of milk. As she followed, she waved her arm toward Marc. It must have been a half minute before he got up from the bench, and then when he did, it seemed he could hardly lift one foot in front of the other. But she knew he would never forgive her if she did not let him make his own way to that door. When he reached it he stood outside a moment, undecided. Danielle stood back, apart, but she could see his grandmother through the window, bending over the soup kettle, and then as he entered, straightening up bravely.

"Marco, my little Marco!" her soft cry came out into the night. It was his baby name, the one his parents and grandparents had used for him, and Danielle was the only one outside of them who had ever had the privilege of calling him that. Now it came to her not only that she had discreetly forborne to use it thus far tonight but that she hadn't once heard him say her own name.

She came in quietly with the bucket of milk. He had sunk into a chair, and Agathe was at his feet taking off his boots. "God is good to this old woman and to this old house. Life comes back with you." She wept, pressing her cheek to the soles of his feet.

"And big!" the grandmother said, getting up again. "Danielle, you did not say he is so big, a head above what Ovide was. We must give you warm milk. There's plenty, plenty. Oh, I could sing tonight!"

At the door, Danielle was letting the tears come out that she'd been holding back. A returned soldier, she thought, should let a couple of women cry a little over him.

His eyes turned toward her. They had looked bleared outside on the road; but even now in their weariness she saw the little lightnings in them they'd used to have. Around his mouth were discolorations from the sores of malnutrition, but his features were mature, deeper cut. He might look thirty kinds of tramp, but he had become a full-grown man.

Agathe pushed a cup of milk into her hands. "Here, Danielle, my chick, let it be a good omen that you bring to his lips the first cup in his home."

Danielle took it and handed it to him. His hand was shaking so badly that she was afraid he'd spill it, and so she helped him carry it to his lips. But he drank only a little.

"That's all I feel like, just now," he said. "If you don't mind, I'm going to bed."

He struggled to get on his feet and fell back into his chair. Danielle came over, a half step, and he clenched a hand on her arm and pulled himself up.

"Thanks," he said bitterly, in disgust at his own weakness.

"I'm the one who should be thankful, Marc."

"What do you mean?" He turned to her fiercely, and yet he was so weak she had to hold him to keep him from falling. As she did so, she felt the rigid shoulder joint under the tunic.

"Just that," she said soothingly. "You may think because you've come home weak and ill, you're going to be dependent on us. But you will get well, and stronger and stronger. Oh, Marco, I need you, I need you!" She dropped her head on his good shoulder and let herself cry. She felt his hand pat her shoulder.

"You mustn't cry, Danielle," he said awkwardly. "It doesn't do any good."

"I know. And especially now, when you're too tired to stay on your feet. But we've become such strangers to each other," she tried to explain.

"Yes, it's true. Three years. We're both of us somebody else. It will take a little time."

He turned and walked slowly toward the bedroom.

8. *Friends in the Clear*

ALTHOUGH the next day was one to work in her own Thirty Rows and she could have taken it off to be with Marc, Danielle was out among her vines shortly after sunup. He would need to sleep late. Nobody in Arsac but the Dufours knew he was back, and if she continued to work as usual, it would be afternoon at least before anyone else would discover that an Arsac hero was home from the war.

Just the same, she had to snatch herself from the wish that he might any moment come out here to Thirty Rows and find her at work. All morning the spell of their strange meeting in the dusk clung to her feelings like strange music, partly sad but mostly wonderful. She couldn't get out of her mind, as she tended her vines, the picture of the pathetic scarecrow figure changing into the gallant friend; the defiant, distrusting look on him becoming wistful and at last familiar and ready for humor.

Every second of it she went over, again and again, like Jeannot when he was little, wanting to have the same story retold. She ate her lunch, with long gazes toward the village. But by two in the afternoon, she could no longer endure staying away from the Bracessac cottage.

The doors were wide open and all was quiet, the dog sleeping on the threshold. Agathe was at the well washing a basket of newly dug potatoes. "He's been asleep most of the time. His fever's about gone. I gave him a bowl of camomile tea after I had him tucked in last night. When he could scarcely open his mouth to take it he said he was afraid he

might become a burden to me, the blessed child."

Across Danielle's heart came the cold dark shadow of the bad news he was to learn; the loss of the Dowry Field and the Bracessac yoke of oxen. "What else, Grandmère did he say about how he feels? Please tell me."

"Well—said he was glad to be under a watertight roof and not have to button his coat tighter to keep the wind out." The old woman saw the thankful gleam in the tall girl's eyes, and so took courage to say: "But this morning he mentioned his arm again, not directly, but worse. He said, he said—" her voice broke, and she burst into tears "this is a two-armed country, he said, the work's all two-armed work, especially his part of it, and I guess he must have meant the Dowry Field." She let the flurry of weeping exhaust itself. Danielle, picking up the basket of potatoes, put an arm around her as they went into the house.

"Has anybody else found out he's home?" Danielle whispered.

"Thanks to Heaven, no! Mathilde was here with some eggs and a squab, and Jeannot—"

"No holding Jeannot, he's heard so much about him."

"Yes," said Agathe, bruising a parsley sprig for the squab, already in the broth, "that's a mania that runs in the Dufour family—" raising her voice, "making so much of the Bracessacs."

"Sssh!"

"Anyhow," the old woman said, returning to a whisper, "he wanted Jeannot to bring the barber. What could you do? Mathilde says, 'I never saw the time a good shave didn't make a man feel better.'—And to think that when he left here he was too young for a razor!—Anyhow as I was saying, Mathilde recommends that Jeannot should go to the barber and say, 'come with me to Monsieur le Curé right away. It's serious.' Then take him to Father Ambrose and tell them, both, the news at the same time, and say that Marc is sick and must have no visitors. Well, it worked like a charm, and along about eleven, here comes Jeannot and the barber with his razor and strop under an arm and with a finger latching his lips shut. 'Tell anybody? Indeed not, Madame.' Did we think he had no professional honor? Then he refused pay. What! To give an Arsac veteran his first shave back home, that too was one of his esteemed privileges. Then he left by the back road to his shop."

"So can I have a peek at Marc?"

"Well, I think his shave has given him enough strength for that. But tiptoe in, my dear, he may be asleep again; it left him a little fatigued."

Danielle stole in. He was asleep. His face seemed wan now, after the shave, and his thinness more pronounced.

She pressed her cheek to his brow, and then stood quietly watching him, letting her eyes feed her whole being on the precious reality of him lying there. After a while his eyes opened to the beam of sunlight that came in upon them. He was unstartled, in his old way. Children used to steal up behind Marc and let out a blood-curdling yell to see if they could make him jump, and he wouldn't even blink. He'd just turn around slowly and smile. It was a gift, like not being ticklish.

"Hello," he said.

"Hello, Marco."

They could think of nothing to say.

He grinned, and she laughed lightly at their mutual inability to talk when there was so much to tell and ask about.

At last he found speech. "Agathe says you were pretty skinny too the day you got back."

"Guess I was. You'll feed up, too. It takes no time at all."

Again one of the strange, unexpected, and overpowering pauses came upon them, when not a thing came to their minds that seemed as worthy of saying as it should be. The ordinary expressions seemed far from good enough.

"I'd like to stay and be a nurse if you'd let me?"

"No thanks. I'd like it. But the barber told me about the vines. They need you more than I do."

She let her head droop and had to say, though she wished she could stop herself: "You don't need me?"

With a broad smile, he raised his head, and patted her arm with the back of his hand, as though he'd sensed the little slip she felt she'd made. "No, Danielle, not for a mere touch of influenza."

So she went back to the vines, letting things be this way between him and herself. She saw him often, of course, but they had a kind of tacit understanding to give each other plenty of time. It was the way, after all, that they were used to doing, a way that the vines had taught them.

After he got up and around, people did not see them together quite so much as they would have expected. There were curious rumors that the loss of the Dowry Field had cooled his ardor, but even those who ventured this notion did not themselves believe it.

It got so that even René began teasing her about him. "You must take his hand like this, and walk down the road—"

"And how do you know I haven't?" she retorted.

"Marc and Danielle," Mama Dumartin explained, "have

been out in the world, and they've learned discretion which we don't have in Arsac, where anybody's business is everybody's. A little privacy, it's the trait of civilization."

Danielle nodded her head to Mama, and winked to René, who was a good sport and understood.

But Papa bowed and said, "My boys, your mother is correct. Children are thoughtless of privacy, but to respect it marks the person of taste." In his genial eyes there was a stern glint.

It seemed that he heartily believed in the principle of maintaining privacy, especially about such matters as where André and he got their sulphate, nitrate of soda, bone meal, and other needs for the vines. But could this source which they called The Co-operative be a sinister thing? No, nobody could look at Papa Dumartin's good big face with its large, fatherly moustache and suspect him of dark dealings.

"What is the matter, why do you look at me so sternly, my Danielle?" he said. "You scare me with your big brown eyes so serious."

"Papa, I'm thinking about my Thirty Rows."

"Oh, that's serious enough."

"Well, is there any privacy about that thing you and André mentioned where you got your sulphate? That— it sounded like 'Co-operative'?"

"Privacy about a co-operative!" he hugged himself for a great laugh. "Lord, no!"

"Well, what is it anyway? Would you tell me?"

"What is it? Only an organization for getting better materials cheaper because everybody does it together, that's all. I'll tell you, my dear, when we get near the time you need chemicals for spring work. We'll see to it that you come in with us."

"Really! Oh, Papa, wait till I tell Marc about this! It will be a tonic to him."

Marc had been able to walk around ably no more than a day or two when he'd asked Felix Dassier for a ride out to the Dowry Field, and both Felix and Victor the blacksmith had to tell him. Marc reported this to Danielle, adding, "Don't worry, we're not going to let them get away with it. A crook never can get all the pieces to fit straight together again."

How he confronted Porky Guichard she had to learn from René, who had been a younger schoolmate of Marc's and still admired everything he did.

"Saturday night, all the folks in the store, standing around, you know. Well, in strolls Marc. Talks to this one, talks to that one, waits his turn for Porky to wait on him. And all the time Porky looks at him out of the corner of his piggy eye. Things got uneasier and uneasier, except for Marc, cool and hard as a gunstock— you don't get to be a sergeant if you're not—well, he watches that dodging pig eye, kind of easily, without seeming to notice it, until, bing! he catches it so Porky has to square his face around at him, and then Marc says, casually, 'Good evening, Monsieur Guichard! Have you kept in good health?' And Porky, he shook his head sadly and said, 'Thank you, but I haven't been so well. We've all had it pretty hard going here.' 'Ah, I'm sorry,' Marc says like his heart was melting on ice. 'Since I have lost the use of this arm and also the use of a little piece of ground I was figuring on, perhaps I could be of some use to you in this business here.' Well! Everybody understood. Imagine Marc working for Porky, or any kind of merchant-work! And, Porky, it was like he had been ducked and was trying to find his breath. 'N-n-no,' he stammers, 'I'm afraid you couldn't.' Everybody knew he had complained of being short of help, and he could see the sneer on their faces."

"Marc's a veteran," I said, "he deserves a job."

"Then Porky blurted out, 'I'm not a welfare organization.' Then Marc smiled and said, 'That's what we all know.' And he walked out."

"This town has had about all it can stand of Guichard," snapped Papa Dumartin, usually gentle-spoken.

Danielle had to learn another thing from René. "Marc has been to see the old army doctor at Macau about his arm. Soak it in hot water, the doctor told him, and knead the muscles. Even though the shoulder is still rigid, if he can limber up the elbow and fingers he can hold the handle of a pitchfork or a hoe, maybe steer a spray-nozzle. I saw Marc last night and he was already proud, because he can bend his elbow about a centimeter or two."

Of course, Marc had very early told her and Agathe very sketchily what had happened to the arm. A truck accident. "The driver went asleep and it rolled off the road down a bank and caught fire. I came out luckier than most of the others—poor fellows!"

Gradually he told more, as the changed, grown-up voices and poised manners of her and himself seemed less and less to be something strange between them.

"While I was shut in behind the barbed wire, all I thought about was getting back home," he said to her one evening, leaning against her cherry tree, "and now I'm here. I'm still trying to believe it."

"And I, Marco," she replied, smiling happily. "Let's not try to believe it for a while, because it's wonderful as it is."

"Now that's the Danielle I thought about in my dreams of home. The one I saw on the road that night—well, I used to see this girl or that girl pass by and I would tell myself she is maybe a little like Danielle, and then I'd say, no, that one is, and none of them would be at all. Then when I did see you, I hadn't eaten for two days and was feeling so miserable I couldn't trust my eyes: I almost thought you were one of those imaginary Danielles. You seemed so suddenly tall, and your face had a different seriousness—a kind of new seriousness about something else, not about you-and-me, no matter what you said."

Then Danielle told him how she too had had fears about him: that he might have outgrown his interest in her and found somebody else. They matched their separate experiences back and forth until both pasts seemed to become a single one.

Again, on a Sunday they were out walking. The first Sunday he had been up he'd been too weak, and the next two he had accompanied his grandmother to Mass and loafed around afterwards with old friends. Danielle chanced by with some of her friends, and he and she managed to exchange split-second smiles that nobody else saw. It kept people guessing, but that didn't matter. On this fourth Sunday the Bracessacs and the Dufours happened to converge homeward from Mass. Marc and Jeannot were walking ahead, discussing airplanes, and the three women followed behind. Before long, though, the formation shifted, and Danielle and Marc found themselves walking together. Marc had on a blue serge suit, made for a heavier man, but it concealed his boniness and gave him a neat, dignified look that made her feel proud.

He began telling her about how his fixed idea of getting home was all that kept him going for a while. "There I was—just one among a million men torn from their homes. We had been licked, and the idea of home and you was like

a point for me to cling to. We were kept moving from camp
to camp, to get away from the other army. That's how the
truck I was in was wrecked, and my wounded shoulder got
bad. I didn't say anything about it, because when you're a
prisoner it's better not to call attention to yourself. When I
strapped my elbow close to my side it didn't ache so much.
I had to sit still and that kept me thinking more than ever
about getting home."

She took his arm as they walked in the clear, kind, home
sunlight: no wonder this had been difficult for him to tell
until now!

"Well, when I got out, something else hit me, like a bomb.
Maimed as I was, what right had I to marry you? I wanted
to die, I was so low. Then a fellow I ran across offered to
help me change my shirt. He stole what money I had. I tried
to get work. They gave me one look: nothing. If I couldn't
support one person how could I support two? Besides, how
did I know you'd want me, after these three years, and the
shape I was in?"

"You were ill, Marco. In health you'd never think that."

"Yes, that's easy enough to see now. Well, I came to a
town, a starving little place. The rain was coming down fit
to drench out the last spark in me. I tell you, I never felt
lower in my life. I went into a poor little church to get dry.
And the priest got me to talking after giving me a roll and
a carrot and some hot vegetable tea in his kitchen, the last
thing I had to eat before I got home. He was on pretty short
rations himself.

"He said if I didn't go home at all I'd be deciding it one
fixed way, and was taking no chances. But if I went home I
was taking chances, and that one of them might be favorable,
that you'd still want me, and that I had no right to do the

deciding first, 'simply out of pride,' he told me, and not give you a chance to decide too. But later, after I took his advice, I got more and more afraid the nearer home I got. I'd have to face your rejecting me, or taking me back because you felt you had to, and I'd not have the strength to say no. I had wanted to wait until I could get a little money and cleaned up first, at least, but this Father, he says no, to go just as I was, and right away. He went out and came back with money for me to eat on while traveling, but I saved it until I'd got near enough so it would buy a ticket to Margaux."

Marc shook Danielle out of the mood this had put her in, as he said, with a chuckle: "And that, Mademoiselle, is the hard-luck story of the tramp you picked up a little while ago along this road."

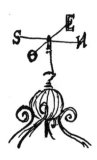

9. *A Letter for Father Ambrose*

"SLAP—whack—slap," went the wooden paddles of the women, beating the soap through the dripping garments they were washing in the Lorina. A weir of logs made the brook balloon out so as to form a tiny lake. The water was still soft from the sky: ideal for washing. It was hard work, but one of the gayest hours of the week. Ripples of laughter rewarded anecdotes, and overhead bees were noisy at their work among the flowers of the lime trees.

The morning was advanced and several of the laundresses had left to stir the fire under the dinner-kettles at home. Into the vacant space next to Mathilde, on the smooth trodden sod, where the bank was reinforced by planking, Agathe moved her knee-box, soap, and bottle of bleaching compound.

"Our young people are taking their time about it," she said, "but they know what they're doing."

Mathilde straightened up where she knelt, to relieve the

muscles of her back. "They will have to be patient, poor dears," she moaned tenderly. "A horse or a pair of oxen are not had for nothing these days."

"Well, Marc knows he can have our next two male calves, but that asks patience too." Agathe plunged at her work.

Mathilde sighed over the Château lingerie she was washing. "We old people compare these hard times with the peaceful abundance we enjoyed as children. We must pray the good Lord that our young ones will find happiness in their own way."

Agathe, growing secretive, peered behind and around. "Shhhh ... Mathilde, listen well to me. My conscience makes me tell you something. I have been afraid, because we are but two lone widows, and we shall have three hard men against us. They are on the town council. I have a cow and three heifers, four goats and a donkey to graze on the town common. If they knew that I know this thing they would prevent me pasturing on the common land. But my conscience gives me no rest."

"What on earth are you mumbling about, Agathe?"

"I owe you seven hundred francs. That is to say, Ovide owed Pierre seven hundred francs. But Ovide will not come back. We hear nothing from Pierre. The matter, therefore, lies between you and me. I speak low that no one may overhear."

"But how does this matter concern three hard men? You speak in riddles, my friend."

"It goes back to the day that our two sons went away," Agathe whispered. "That last afternoon Ovide went with Pierre when he sold his wine. Afterward they went to Guichard's to settle their bills with him. Ovide owed twelve hundred francs but he only had five hundred. Pierre loaned him the difference after having paid his own bill. When Ovide came into the house he told me. 'Mama,' he said, 'I have paid Guichard, but I had to borrow seven hundred of Pierre to do it.'"

"This is good news, Agathe. Is it true?"

"By the head of my father, word for word, it is as I tell you." Mme. Bracessac scrubbed for a few moments, until a loiterer passed. "I do not have the money at once, but I thought that I might give you a heifer and a couple of goats. One goat is in milk and the other freshens in a month."

"It is agreed and I thank you, but I still don't understand where the three hard men come in."

"But surely you see where this leads us, and why I am afraid. If Pierre paid Guichard his bill he owed the pig nothing. Guichard had no right to seize your land. He can be put in prison for dishonesty. If Ovide were alive, he would be your witness. Guichard knew that and did not move on the land matter until I had the official letter saying that Ovide was dead. Guichard's safety depends upon this thing that we know not becoming public. If we speak we shall have Guichard, Maître Blanchard and Roger l'Eglise who farms the field fighting us."

"What you say is what Danielle also says," Mathilde nodded in agreement. "Danielle heard Pierre tell Jeanne that he had paid everything and that is why the girl will not give up faith in getting her Field back."

"All we can do," Mathilde counselled presently, "is to keep our ears open and our mouths shut. *Le lion Dieu* makes justice to come in the end."

With that the two women shook hands. A momentous secret was between them.

They piled their knee-boxes upon their wheelbarrows, arranged the paddles and the wet wash within the boxes, shook hands again, tapped the sand out of their sabots, and went their different ways.

That evening Danielle was hunched over the fire, thinking. The grandmère was putting her chickens to bed, and Jeannot was feeding turnip tops to his own personal rabbit. The table was laid and they would soon be in for supper. Her Marc had been home a month now, and they had talked themselves out over such a variety of subjects that she could never be sure whether she was reviewing his thoughts or her own.

Shuffling steps approached the front of the house. "Why, it's Monsieur le Curé!" she cried, jumping up. "What an honor you do us." The venerable priest was apparently feeling well but out of breath and welcomed the chair she set for him. "You shouldn't have made the effort, Father."

In his hand was an envelope, and when he had regained his breath he drew forth the contents.

"It came late, after the postman had finished his rounds, but Mme. Lafon, noticing the foreign stamp and thinking it might be urgent, sent it along by the bread boy."

Mathilde and Jeannot came in, shook hands, and listened.

"There are two letters in the envelope, the short one for me and the longer one for Danielle. They are from Jeanne."

"She is alive then," cried the girl. "*Le bon Dieu* be praised."
She threw her arms about her brother and Mathilde. "And
my father?"

"Alive too, I believe. Folded in my letter is the one for
you. I will read you mine." Danielle had lighted the candle
and set it near his elbow.

Dear Father Ambrose:

*Despite your advancing age I pray that you may still be
in charge of the parish at Arsac-le-Petit, and that, if you
are, you may know of some way of communicating with
my family.*

*In the past I have written to many addresses, without
reply. I am sending copies of the enclosed letter to four places
in the hope that someone may have trace of my family. The
last I knew they were in the Midi with no known address.
It is of the greatest importance that Danielle receive the
enclosed copy. With thanks and respectful salutations, I
remain gratefully,*

Jeanne Dufour

"I would suggest, my child," said the old man, "that you
read your letter first to yourself, then aloud to us."

Danielle had barely fastened her eyes upon the page before her cheeks were wet with tears. "Don't mind my crying.
These are tears of joy. They are together and want to come
home. Oh, my Jeannot, you will see our Papa and Mama."
More in command of herself, she said, "Here is what my
mother writes:"

My Little Girl:

But you will be a big girl now. I write you among many anxieties but with a heart full of love, thanking God that we have you, for it will be you alone who can bring Pierre home.

I was injured in an attack on the factory where I worked. In the hospital I caught a low fever, like the workers all had, and wasted away until I could walk but a few steps. They told me to get home and I was in the railroad station when I saw a face I knew. It was a teamster of Château Monbrison, who, going through a hospital, had seen Pierre. I only saw the man a minute in the station but he gave me Pierre's address. Papa was near to death. He did not know me at first, but I felt that with food and love I could save him.

I got him to the house of a peasant woman I had come to know. The peasants are the only ones who have food in this country. Her men were killed so she had a room. The hospital let Papa go because they thought him the same as dead. For two months we have been at Anna's house. He is better but he will not be really well until we can get him home. I owe Anna a great deal of money, the prices here you would not believe. She is angry because I have not paid her and may bring in the police. If they put us in a camp again we shall never live to get home.

Danielle, this is what you must do. Follow my directions exactly. You must bring 5,000 francs. I do not know where you can get so much, someone may loan it. Fold the thousand franc notes lengthwise and sew them inside the waistband of your skirt. Keep out seven hundred francs for your journey. On the train talk to no one. Let no one know that you have money. Trust no one. The women are worse than the men. Men in soldier uniform are the worst. If you must ask questions ask only of men in police or railway uniforms. If they ask where you are going, say that you are joining your family. Many are doing that.

Print these directions upon strong paper and sew them upon your shoulder where all can read.

TO PARIS. TO STRASBOURG. TO MANNHEIM. TO KATZENBUCKEL.

Leave train at Katzenbuckel, go eight kilometers to Lazarett Am Thuringer Wald (Hospital in the woods). Follow the road straight past the hospital for one kilometer to two cedars on the left. Path between the cedars goes 200 meters to Anna's house.

I am counting on you. Without the 5,000 francs we shall not get out of here alive. I will go to the post office with these four letters, then to the church, light a candle before the altar and say a prayer that one of these letters reach you. With all tenderness to Jeannot and the grandmother,

Your mother,

Jeanne Dufour

After Danielle had finished reading, the priest, the two women, and the boy sat in silence for many minutes. The intense earnestness of the mother's words had taken them out of themselves. They in imagination walked past the hospital, stopped between the two cedars, found Pierre's bed in Anna's little house.

"You will go? All that she says, you will do, yes?" The old man studied the girl, who nodded. "Good. Now I must get to my soup, or Sister Hermaline will think the devil has stolen me. Jeannot will be a good boy and accompany me with the lantern."

The girl came out of her brown study. "Excuse me, Father, I go tomorrow, but it will be prudent if others do not know the news until I am gone. You will please to keep this even from the good Sister Hermaline."

His blue eyes had a twinkle. "Rest assured, my child." He had a final word for them: "May God give peace to this house and to those within it."

Danielle ate little and withdrew to the cherry tree. She was glad that she had thought to warn the priest. In Arsac such information spread like a sunburst. She cudgelled her wits to think of some means other than the notary, to raise the money. And if Maître Blanchard suspected that Pierre were alive he would certainly refuse to hand the funds to another than the head of the family. She and Mathilde must be at his office the first hour of the morning, and meanwhile he must have no inkling of Jeanne's letter or the projected journey.

The necessity of closing the door upon the possibility of sometime regaining the Dowry Field was more of a blow to Danielle than if it had happened earlier. For the dream was beginning to assume substance. She, Mathilde and Jeannot were living within their earnings, were even saving steadily. With the six thousand francs at the notary's as a nest egg, it was not unreasonable to cherish hopes.

She and Marc had once sat under the live oak, let the loam sift through their fingers. Other land the Dufours and the Bracessacs had, but no other comparable in richness. The boy and girl had seen themselves going out with the dew on the foliage, resting the lazy-nooning, returning at night with the cart piled high with food: potatoes to roast in the ashes, leeks and beans for the soup, corn for the clucking flock around their ankles. A right and a sound life could be built around the Field. To sign the quitclaim would irrevocably close the door to all right to sue for its return.

But on the other side of the balance was the return of Pierre—curly-headed, black-eyed Pierre, ready to laugh with anyone, ready to help anyone. To have him back again, in time to have him big-muscled and tanned again, what could compare with that joy. Once she had brought the issue out into the open, and stated it nakedly like that—to have Pierre back, or to have the Field—it was no issue at all. Of course the Field must go. She hated herself to have even seemed to hesitate. She would run into the house to remind Mathilde again that the glad tidings must be bottled up until the morning, and then she would find Marc. For the disposition of the Field was partly his business, just as the exercises and treatment of his shoulder (as he now could understand) was partly her business.

She walked rapidly down the Margaux road and across the fields. Through the opening doorway she could see Agathe knitting and Marc whittling a scythe handle. At her whistle he joined her.

"I was expecting you," he said. "It's funny, but all the evening I've had a sort of premonition that something was going to happen. Tell me quick, what is it?"

"Marc, it's the biggest news we could have. Father and Mother are alive, but far off and sick. Pierre is the sickest. Jeanne says that I'm to come with money and bring them home. I'm to go tomorrow but no one must know until after I've left." She related the events of the last hour. When she told him about the necessity of renouncing all claims on the Dowry Field, there was a lump in her throat.

Marc nodded understandingly. "Of course. Of course. Nothing counts but to get him back."

"You're such a comfort," she whispered as they walked along. "If I ever disagree with you, I'll be pretty sure that I'm wrong."

"You are wrong now—about one part of your plan, Danielle. It is altogether unsuitable that you go. Your mother is right in warning you to trust no one you meet. She might have made it stronger. There are thousands of people in that starving, outlaw country who would think no more of killing you than of eating an apple. There are half-grown children who would cut your throat and throw you in a ditch for half a loaf of bread. Of course there are good-hearted people, like this Anna, but the ones who frequent the roads and hang around railroad stations are human weasels and wolves. No, no, my girl, someone will go tomorrow, but it won't be you. I'm the one who goes." They had come to a standstill, close together, she listening, bewildered. Marc seemed absolutely positive.

"I'm not even sure that the railroad would sell you a ticket once you are across the frontier. I've picked up a few words of their language. I have a hospital discharge from that same region, and here's the frozen shoulder to prove it. In my sloppy old uniform I'll be one of the penniless vagabonds they see by the hundred every day. No one will look at me twice. And as to thinking that I had as much money as ten francs, they'd hoot. I'll say that I'm trying to track down my lost relatives.

"Why, Danielle," he exclaimed with waxing enthusiasm, "if we'd been getting me ready to take on this job, we couldn't have planned it any better." He could see that she was weakening. She was impressed by his arguments, and his assurance was contagious.

"Is it a bargain, Danielle?"

"I suppose so, although it does seem like walking out on Mother."

"No you're not. What she needs is someone who will get the money to her safely and quickly, and then give them a hand in getting Pierre home. I can carry the money safer than you. And I can take it cheaper than you, for on some parts of the trip, I can ride on the platforms or roofs of cars where they don't even ask an invalid soldier for a ticket. We'll sew the bills inside the waistband of my trousers."

There were stars in her eyes. "Marco, Marco, what would I do without you?"

Maître Blanchard himself opened the door to his early callers and showed Mathilde and Danielle into his office.

Danielle stated their errand and his lips curled in a superior smirk.

"So you've at last come to your senses, young lady. It's about time." As a matter of fact the notary was more relieved to have the suit definitely closed than he wanted them to know. People had begun to be inquisitive as to why a soldier on service had not been protected by the moratorium. Without hesitation he counted out the crisp notes and had the two women sign a general release. A few hours later—when the village was buzzing over Jeanne's letter—he would have time to wonder whether he had not been a trifle impetuous.

Before the sun was quite at the meridian Danielle and Marc set out for Macau. She would walk with him to the crossroad where he caught the bus for Bordeaux. They had never felt so close together. He was on an adventure that involved separation, but he was going as the representative of the new family—his and hers. The money was safely sewed out of sight. In his musette, to whet Pierre's appetite, were six little cheeses, the first that Mathilde had made of milk from the Bracessac goats. He was not to be distinguished from any other soldier boy at loose ends, save by the purposeful glint in his eye. Danielle clung to him.

"You will telegraph the day and the hour you get to Margaux. We'll borrow the Widow Hourdibaight's carryall and meet you. You'd better address the message to Monsieur le Curé, they'll be more particular in delivering it." The motor swung around the curve. He held her in one of his rare kisses.

She felt small and alone as the bus roared away. Obeying a compulsion which she did not attempt to explain, she walked straight to the Dowry Field, and cried herself out, lying between the roots of the live oak. Under the afternoon haze the Field had never seemed so verdantly opulent. She knew that she had come to say goodbye to something very dear. For good and all, she had padlocked the door.

"How foolish I am." She was winking fast to dry her eyes, and was speaking to the Field. "Things turn out better than we could arrange them. If Guichard hadn't stolen you from me, I shouldn't have had the money to bring my father home. I'm glad that I had you to give."

10. *The Dufour Dander Is Up*

EIGHT days had passed since Marc's departure. It had been a hectic week for Danielle and Mathilde; in addition to their work at the Dumartins' and for the Château, they had tried to think of everything that would make the place more attractive for the home-coming parents. The interior walls and ceilings were brushed down, the floors scrubbed with sand. Pierre's big bed was aired and made. The last of the firewood, which the sawmill contractor had donated, was bound into faggots

and stowed under cover with the help of Agathe's donkey. Jeannot had cleaned his rabbit cage and combed the long-suffering Bergère. Half the garden had been planted to quick-growing salads, leeks and spinach. Spurred by their desire to have everything alluring to the eye they allowed an extravagance—nothing less than having the house whitewashed. But it was worth it. "Simply for the joy to come home to," declared Danielle.

Madame Hourdibaight had refused to entrust her horse to a girl; so it was arranged for Victor to do the driving. They would spread a mattress upon the floor of the carryall and have plenty of blankets. Mathilde would be waiting with a strengthening drink—two eggs beaten up in a glass of milk.

Danielle had a letter from Marc. It was fortunate, he said, that she had not come, since the military police would have stopped her at the frontier. Even Jeanne, when she had taken stock of traveling conditions, admitted that she had made a mistake in asking the girl to come alone. Jeanne was curious as to where the money had come from, insisting upon being told. So far, Marc said, he had put her off.

Pierre—Marc went on to say—was painfully thin and

bloodless. Danielle must be prepared for a shock. Marc was touched by the way the older man clung to him. It seemed as though he accepted Ovide's son as a substitute for his lifelong friend. At the Katzenbuckel station there was a ticket seller who spoke French, and whose mother, even, was born in the southwestern wine country. That made an immediate bond between them, and he had helped them arrange their trip.

They would leave on Wednesday morning, since on Wednesday was held the public market, where Anna's cousin sold vegetables. The cousin would bring Pierre and Jeanne into Katzenbuckel along with her produce. They would spend the first night at Strasbourg, where the Red Cross, in the main waiting room, had established a dormitory for ailing travelers, and sold soup, with bread, very cheaply. By this schedule they would get to Margaux by the late train on Friday. He would telegraph if there was any change.

With the often-read letter upon her knee, and her feet swinging free under the cherry tree seat, Danielle closed her eyes and pictured what it would be like, that first evening at home, with the five Dufours around the supper table; what Jeanne would say, what Mathilde would say. She herself would be saying very little. She would simply be sitting close to Pierre, stroking his hand. Jeannot, in his new sabots, would come clumping in from Blanche's stable, holding the milk pitcher high, not to spill a drop. Mathilde would steal out to the dark room to bring in the double-size cheese she had made for the occasion. Jeanne would be leaning over the fire, ladling out the soup that had been simmering since noon. These were the unnoticed, everyday things that she had taken for granted a thousand times but had missed since the war. Now, if anybody should ask her, they were the most precious things to want out of life.

Friday afternoon came at last. Danielle was glad that Marc had forewarned her, for she would hardly have known her father. Victor gathered him up as though he were a bundle of faggots, laid him on the mattress, wrapped him in blankets. He let the horse walk, Jeanne sitting beside Pierre. Marc and Danielle, hand-in-hand, walked behind, their eyes on one another, completely happy.

"She'll ask about the money as soon as she gets you alone," Marc warned. "She finds it unbelievable that you should get her letter in the evening and that I should be on the road the next morning, with the bills sewed in. I think that she has a thousand francs left."

He related incidents of the trip, comparing the two countries. "We think our towns are quiet, but over there they are stone dead and buried. No one goes out at night because of prowlers. They cut off girls' hair. They will steal the shirt off your back and the shoes off your feet. *Mon Dieu*, I'm glad to get away from those cold, grey, clammy places. I never want to live anywhere but in Arsac-le-Petit."

They had come to the opening in the hedge, the short-cut across the field to Marc's grandmother's. "They've seen enough of me for a while," he said. "Victor can carry him in. You'll like to be by yourselves, without outsiders."

Danielle smiled at him. "But you're not an outsider."

"I'd like you to think that I'm not. Good night."

The first meal of the united Dufour family was as Danielle had pictured it. After the convalescent was tucked in bed and the house was quiet Jeanne took her daughter by the arm and led her into a corner. "Now, my girl, you're going to tell me where you got all that money, and how you got it so quick."

Beginning with Guichard's robbing of Mathilde over the cow and goats, Danielle told the whole story. "It seemed like signing the death warrant of a member of the family, to sign that quitclaim, but what would you? I couldn't see any other way."

"My poor, brave girl!" Jeanne's anger had been rising by the minute. "I never heard anything so disgusting as that Guichard. He was always hungry for money, and has cheated people in his small, chiseling ways, on what they bought at his store, the weight, the price, the quality. But cheating on the Dowry Field is criminal. Pierre did not owe him a cent. Porky can go to jail for this."

"And Papa, when he learns, he'll go out of his head," Danielle reflected.

"We must keep Papa from knowing of it," said Jeanne decisively. "Anyway, until he gets solidly upon his feet. If he had known of this when he was at his lowest . . . well . . . we shouldn't all be here tonight. We'll warn the people he's likely to see."

The ensuing month Pierre drank deep of the tonic of dreamless sleep. A thin slice of his mother's cheese, wrapped in lettuce leaves, imparted something to his vitals that a tubful of hospital gruel never had. Day-to-day milestones marked upward steps in vigor; the day he walked around the Place on his wife's arm; the day he tramped off without a cane, a hint of the juvenile swing to his elbow; the day he first lifted and swung a hoe. How they laughed and cried over each step forward!

But Jeanne and Danielle need not have worried as to how they might, most tactfully, divulge the bad news of the Dowry Field. It was taken out of their hands. Leon Ruhle, who lived out beyond Ligondra, and who had not been initiated into the conspiracy of beneficent silence, strode up to the armchair in which Pierre was sunning himself. He shook hands and spilled the beans magnificently. "Old fellow, we are all in sympathy with you. It was a dirty trick the storekeeper played." Pierre looked blank as Leon resumed his way.

The man had sown a seed. Pierre brooded over his remark. Did he refer to Pierre's imprisonment, or to the slowness of his recovery? But in neither of these did the storekeeper play a part.

"Come here a moment, Jeanne," he called to his wife.

As a loyal partner Jeanne held nothing back. She retold the story of Guichard's treachery, with Mathilde, with him; the sale of the Field and the final forfeiture, by Mathilde and Danielle, of their right to reopen the suit. For the moment Pierre was stunned.

By the time she had finished he was in a white hot fury. "The contemptible liar. He made the whole thing up out of his head. I don't owe him a single sou. And, almost worse than losing the Field, is being branded as a man who would walk out on his obligations. What must the neighbors think of me?" Pierre's disposition being forthright and vehement, he knew of no way to meet injustice save by a head-on collision. "Give me my stick," he snorted, "I'll have it out with that bandit, face-to-face."

"No, no, Pierre," pleaded Jeanne. "Please, please, don't be rash. Guichard did this according to law, and we must undo it according to law. We can find a way if you are intelligent, and you will have a better revenge. Let me call in Victor. He is an honest man and he is our friend. He followed all the steps."

Pierre was listening, so his wife was encouraged to make

another point. "He may have robbed others, too. When dishonest men make money easily, it tempts them further. Guichard succeeded in robbing Mathilde. He robbed you. Who knows how many others? Let us be prudent, gather our information with care. Who knows but in getting fair play for ourselves we may help some other victim as well?" Pacified but still unconvinced, Pierre subsided into his chair.

For two hours Victor answered questions. The conclusion to which he brought Pierre was that, if he were unable to prove that he did not owe the original debt, the Field was permanently lost.

"If Ovide were only here, if Ovide were only here," Pierre repeated vainly. "He saw me count the notes into Porky's hand. He saw Porky nod when I said, 'This leaves me square with the book.' If Ovide were here he could send that rascal where he belongs. Then, quick enough, the timid ones would come forward with their stories."

Then came a morning when Pierre's sense of injury and frustration weighed intolerably upon him. It was not in his nature to submit to injustice like a slinking rabbit. The women were at work in the fields, otherwise they would have restrained him.

He pushed his felt slippers into his sabots, grasped his cane, strode across the Place de la République. There were other customers in the store, but business came to a dead end with Pierre's first word,

"What's this I hear about you swearing that I owed you a three-year-old account when I went into the army? That's a lie, and you know it. I have never let a bill run more than two months. The day I was called up I stood where I stand now, and paid every centime I owed. It was the sixth of November, the day I sold my crop to Château Cantenac, and I paid twenty-two hundred and fifty francs. Ovide Bracessac was with me and he paid twelve hundred francs, of which I loaned him seven hundred. Do you deny any of what I say?" He paused, breathing belligerently through his nose.

"Shhhh . . ." hissed Porky, leaning over the counter, "Someone will hear you."

"I want them to hear me." Pierre's voice was louder than ever. "I want every mother's son in this town to get the rights of this. I want them to know the sort of slimy double crosser you are. You believed the report that Ovide was dead and that I was dead. You dug up old accounts to rob women and children. I don't know a name contemptible enough for you. I'm not dead. I'm here to accuse you to your fat face."

Pierre felt better, like a man who has given his soul a bath. Awed silence had descended upon the store. The two men bent toward one another. Porky's bald head, on his short neck, was swelled crimson. "Get out of my store," he goggled, "get out and stay out."

"Not until I've had my say. I don't yet know how far Blanchard is mixed up in this. You must have paid him a fat fee to have him shave the corners of the law against an absent soldier."

Guichard was struggling to preserve some remnant of his dignity. "My books are regularly kept, showing articles, prices and dates. You must have a receipt, duly stamped, for all payments made."

"Ha, ha! You pulled that bluff on Mathilde about her cow. Receipts duly stamped. How likely! You are the one who has refused to give stamps. Stamps cost a franc apiece, and you're too stingy to furnish them, though the law requires it. Everyone here knows that you've never given stamped receipts."

The people in the store regarded Pierre with frank curiosity. The man had courage, but no prudence. He was enjoying himself, but at a bold price. None of them liked or trusted Guichard, but his was the only store in the village. The nearest competitor was three miles distant. Practically speaking, Arsac people were obliged to pay Porky's prices, accept his short weight and mediocre merchandise, or to go without. Therefore, although the listeners applauded Pierre's spirit they could not compliment his good sense.

But Pierre had not quite finished. "I'll go, but I can't help wondering how many dead men, and how many families of dead men, you have plundered as you plundered me. People hereabouts are afraid to stand up to you. But once I get you on the run, there'll be plenty to join in the chase. You'll probably get a life sentence, at hard labor. It will make Arsac a healthier place."

Prodded beyond endurance, Porky slammed a grain scoop upon the counter and shook his fist. "Enough loose talk, Pierre Dufour. I've been patient because you've been a sick man. But this goes too far. You have questioned my character before my customers. The law has a remedy for libel. We shall see if you do not sing small when I get you in court. Now again I say, get out and stay out."

Pierre was feeling wonderful. For once he had told Porky just what he thought of him. He was riding the crest of the wave. But he was conscious of a shocked silence behind him, and of feet shuffling toward the wall. He turned. Maître Blanchard was inside the door.

"I heard what you said, Dufour. Not all of it, but enough to build a case of defamation of character," said the lawyer frigidly. "The persons present will be our witnesses. For once your big mouth and your temper have landed you in serious trouble. You have no evidence to stand on, either in a slander suit, or in your claim that the land was unjustly seized. You seem to forget that it was your own representatives, who, of their free will and after full consideration, signed the quit-claim. You'd better take Monsieur Guichard's advice to get out and stay out."

As the notary began writing down the names of those who had overheard the squabble, Pierre faded away. Gone was his mood of triumph at being able to bawl Porky out. Instead he was terribly uneasy. What had his rash visit let him in for? It would mean more money, more bad blood, a long-drawn fight. Jeanne would give him the rough side of her tongue when she got home. And for once he would deserve it.

When Danielle came home to dinner, Pierre had finished his confession, and Jeanne was repeating wearily, "Of course, you are right. Every word you said is true. But he has the only store. Where does it get us? It means that Marc will have to buy our groceries for us, or that I shall have to walk three miles to Prosper's, and three miles back. My Pierre, I love you, but you don't help things. Can't you understand that we are at his mercy?"

Pierre looked wretchedly deflated.

With her mother's words ringing in her ears like a funeral dirge, Danielle ate hurriedly and retreated to the cherry tree. "Will I never hear the last of that," she sighed. "Since my cradle how many thousand times have I heard it, 'We are at his mercy.' "

But this time the complaint bounced right back. It bounced back squarely into her face, like a rubber ball. Moreover, it bounced back in the form of a question. "We are at his mercy, but do we need to be? Have we ever lifted one little finger not to be?"

Her dangling feet swung faster as her thought gathered momentum. Arsac wasn't unique, it wasn't the only place with a Guichard. And did all these one-store towns just sit back and submit to the abuse year after year? It was unthinkable. She'd been around the country and seen people; they weren't all without spirit. She'd seen people who wouldn't stand for anything like this, not for ten days even. They'd object, they'd get together and—

Her feet stopped swinging. They'd get together and buy all their groceries somewhere else, even if they had to borrow a truck or a wagon and go ten kilometers for it. They'd do the same for their groceries as the Dumartins did for their farm supplies.

She sat up with a gratified smile and scratched the back of her neck against the tree trunk.

This was something to investigate. If that Co-operative could get bluestone why couldn't it get flour? And sugar. And matches. And lamp oil. And soap, and, and . . .

She leapt out of the tree and skipped to the barn, where her father was leaning over the workbench, re-fitting a hoe-handle. "Don't be too downcast, my little Pierre," she said. "It did you good to blow up like that. I love it in you. And who knows but it may set some of the other customers to thinking!"

11. *The Only Way to Find Out*

NEXT morning she took her blue wool dress from its hanger and slipped it over her head.

"Vivette has promised me a nice ride on her bike, Mama, and this morning I feel like taking it. Papa has been looking a few of the vines over for himself every day; so I don't feel guilty running away."

Jeanne nodded. "It will do you both good. You need the recreation and he the meditation, over his impetuousness. The leaping Dufours! They leap, then they look. Goodbye, dear, enjoy yourself."

Danielle pedalled over to the Dumartins. The men were all away. She exchanged some gossip with Mama, and struck out for the nine kilometers to Castelnau to see André, Arlette's husband.

He was harrowing a vineyard on the further outskirts of the town.

"Well, well, well!" he exclaimed, and then seeing the

serious look on her face after her first smile of greeting: "Hope no trouble brings you here, Danielle?"

"Well, yes, it's trouble," she reflected.

"Tst-tst! I'm sorry," he said sympathetically as he beat the dust off his arms and came toward her. "I hope I can be of service."

"I hope so too, André," she said. "I have to know something about that Co-operative of yours."

Greatly relieved, he laughed, "I'm not the one to tell you, Danielle, except that it's organized buying, and I've found it good. The right man to tell you about it is the organizer. Hm-hm-hmph!" he said, shaking his head. "I wondered how long it would be before the mutton-heads at Arsac woke up. That Guichard has you people following him around like sheep, and you don't do anything but bleat. When Papa Dumartin and I once even so little as mentioned the idea of a Co-operative to a few of the village, they threw up their hands and said it savored of conspiracy."

"Excuse me," Danielle corrected, "I didn't say that Arsac sends me here and wants to know—"

"Then it's no use, no use. Sorry."

"Would you be so kind as to keep this visit confidential? Thanks. And also, would you tell me who the organizer is and where I can find him?"

"Don't get angry," said André companionably, "I meant no harm." He took her by the arm and led her past his horse's head. "See the house with the cupola yonder? M. Delor lives there. He'll talk your ears off unless they're sewed on tight; but he knows what he's talking about."

Danielle warmed to M. Delor at once. He was a pint-sized man with a pointed white beard. She had no sooner disclosed her errand than he leaped upon his hobby and was off. He was easy to talk with because he did all the talking himself. Like many an enthusiast he would ask a question, then, without pause, proceed to answer it.

"Perfectly, Mademoiselle, I understand your meaning. Can Arsac-le-Petit enjoy the benefits of a Co-opérative Agricole it can indeed. Is the Co-operative Movement going strong indeed it is eighty new branches in the Department and not yet three years old." Delor then hurled himself into what Danielle guessed to be an oft-repeated public speech. But it told her what she had come to find out.

"How do we go about it, Mademoiselle? Well, here are some pamphlets which give precise information. I'll wrap up a dozen of them for you to circulate. The first step will be a meeting in the Arsac schoolhouse, and your responsibility will be to have as many landowners, men or women, present as possible. Sunday afternoon will be the best time, when the men will not be at work. I will make a speech, telling the whole story." His face glowed with amused anticipation. "I am pretty good at this sort of thing, if I do say it myself, that's why I'm the Departmental organizer.

"We require ten or more landowners as charter members. Each member contributes three hundred francs toward the working capital, and the government— which encourages our movement—makes an advance up to fifty thousand francs, without interest. We thus have a rolling fund with which to carry on the business. We elect an executive committee of five members who make the purchases and approve the names of members who want to run a charge account. The local committee must provide a warehouse to store supplies, and it appoints a secretary-treasurer who keeps accounts and makes sales. You buy goods at wholesale from manufacturers and sell at cost, dealing in all articles used on a farm or in a farm home. You would hardly believe what an economy it is, as well as getting fresher, better-quality and honest-weight goods. It is no wonder that hundreds of Co-ops are springing up all over France.

"But my compliments to you, Mademoiselle, for your public spirit. You certainly have the matter at heart to ride nine kilometers on a sultry afternoon. Pardon me, while I call my wife, that she may offer you a slight refreshment. Come again when you have set a date for the first meeting. I will be there and will bring a couple of our Castelnau members to testify to their personal experience in our Co-op."

Danielle was cheered by her call. There didn't seem to be any obstacle to the organization of a Co-operative in Arsac. Now for stirring up sentiment in favor of the meeting. The simplest way would be to have a committee, say of four—Marc and Vivette, and perhaps René Dumartin, to talk up the meeting and pass the pamphlets about.

On her way to return the bicycle Danielle paused at the Bracessacs' to have Agathe send Marc to Vivette's.

The two girls seated themselves under the lime trees behind the wine cellar and Danielle untied the bundles of pamphlets. "You don't know where I've been." She then told Vivette everything.

With Marc's appearance Danielle went over the high spots, and they began to study the reading matter. "M. Delor gave me some posters to tack up on the bulletin boards of the post office and the mayor's. We can have the first meeting on a week from Sunday, that will give us time to talk it up . . ."

"We'll have to see the schoolmaster for permission to use the room," said Marc, "and he'll tell the pupils to urge their parents to attend. I'm afraid the oldtimers of Arsac will say they've gotten along all these years without any sort of co-operation, and still can."

He was searching his memory for something. "Ah, I've got it. Long ago there was a mutual-benefit insurance and burying society. It worked nicely—until the treasurer left with the funds. Some of our old people will repeat the story and say, 'No thank you, not again.' All the same, I think you're on the right track, Danielle."

Aside from issuing oral invitations, arranging with the schoolmaster to preside and introduce M. Delor, there wasn't a great deal that the committee could do during the next week. "About every second person I talk to says, 'What will Porky Guichard think of all this?'" René reported. "He has a lot of influence among those who owe him money. He'll show fight before losing his trade, and you know he's a dirty fighter."

"All right, let him *show* fight," said Marc, "let's force him out into the open. He's been able to do his dirty work unseen, because we've been asleep. The fat crook looks me up and down sort of sneering, as though he had a secret joke on me."

The weather was fine, that Sunday afternoon, and the schoolroom was jam-packed. The Committee of Four was pleased to see not only the young people but the solid taxpayers who would meet the requirements for membership. The schoolmaster introduced M. Delor and turned the meeting over to him. The little man was as eager as a boy in an orchard; he went around shaking hands with acquaintances, brimful of pleasantries.

He kept the jovial air even when he began his speech, giving an analysis of the peasant's character, its strength and its weakness. But the weakness which most seriously retarded the peasant's prosperity, M. Delor said, was his individualism and his suspiciousness. Experience had taught him to trust no one but himself. The great landowners were hungry to gobble up his fields. Wholesalers deceived him as to prices. The government piled up taxes and drafted his sons for the army. The politicians made honeyed promises which they never intended to fulfil. No wonder he was suspicious, of banks, of government, even of his fellow farmers. But he carried individualism too far when he refused to unite with his fellow peasants in co-operative buying and selling. Isolated they were weak, united they could dominate the situation. "What I recommend to you, I see demonstrated every day of my life," he concluded.

Two members of the Castelnau Co-op followed, with personal experiences of their organization's benefits. Questions were asked and answered.

Porky Guichard had the nerve to come. He arrived late and plumped himself down in the front row. One thing must have affected him deeply. When M. Delor was speaking of the economies achieved by a Co-op, he handed round mimeographed sheets giving the pricelist of the various articles. The difference between the Guichard prices and the Co-op prices was staggering.

When people saw the scandalous profit Porky must be making they looked at him, expecting some explanation or comment. His piggy eyes glittered, the red crawled up to his bald head, he rose and stamped from the school without a word. It was inevitable that the audience should titter.

The schoolmaster proposed a vote of thanks to M. Delor and the out-of-town speakers, and gave notice of the meeting for the following Sunday. Today's meeting had been to prepare the soil, he said, and give information, but the real business was for the second assembly, when the Arsac Co-opérative Agricole would really become a going business. Only proprietors of farms, men or women, were invited. They must be prepared to deposit their membership fee of three hundred francs, and to sign the constitution. They would elect an executive committee which would manage the society, and appoint a secretary-treasurer.

Still smiling over Porky's withdrawal, and with a buzz of good feeling, the audience adjourned. More than one shook hands with the Committee of Four saying that Arsac needed to co-operate in many community improvements and this was a fine beginning.

During the evening Marc knocked at the Dufour door, and entered grinning broadly. "We've got the old thief on the run," he said. "Our next meeting has got his wind up. He has actually offered me a job, to open a new branch of his business, to drive round and take orders and deliver the goods, a route in all the nearby villages. You see? Already he wants to buy me away from the Co-op. Always the crooked way. Oh yes, he says he's going to double his stock, and have weekly bargain sales on special goods. He's going to enlarge the store and carry clothing and shoes. You'd die to hear him. I didn't say no, outright, because I want to keep track of his projects."

During the week the Committee of Four rested on their laurels. There would only be the book work and taking in the subscription money. Nothing happened in any of the families of the Committee, but Agathe remarked to Marc that there seemed to be a lot of low-voiced discussion going on in the store, that suddenly stopped when she entered. "I feel in my bones that something is going on."

"Maybe so," agreed Marc carelessly. "Within six months

the Co-op will have him sewed up tight."

In this mood of easy self-confidence the Committee awaited the business meeting.

It put Vivette in a pretty flurry. "M. Delor said that the voting would be by paper ballots. How many do you think I should get ready. Fifty?"

"Yes, fifty or sixty, will be about right," replied Danielle, with ten other things on her mind. "We can make extra ones at the last minute."

M. Delor came a little early to write out the order of business on the blackboard. Vivette's uncle, a retired major of the infantry came next, then the Dumartins, Pierre and Jeanne, and Agathe Bracessac. They sat about, exchanging optimistic comments.

M. Delor kept looking out the window and snapping his watch. "It's very odd, very odd. I heard the professor give the notice properly. But there isn't anyone in sight and it's half an hour past the announced time."

"They certainly meant to come—or at least I thought they did," said Danielle, baffled.

The Committee of Four and their loyal supporters waited another half-hour. No one appeared.

The Departmental organizer left, implying by his manner that the Committee had been guilty of some discourtesy. The families drifted away, disappointed, not saying much, consumed by curiosity. Vivette went with her uncle.

At length René, Marc, and Danielle were alone in the deserted schoolroom. They wearied their wits trying to answer the riddle.

"I'd cry if I weren't so mad," said the girl.

Marc was thinking out loud, in the slow way he had. "It took something powerful to keep away a whole crowd like that. And it was done on the quiet, so none of us would know."

"I've just thought of something," said René. "Yesterday that cocky Louis Fort was making remarks. He's just a nitwit, so I didn't pay attention. But his mother is the sister of Porky Guichard's wife. I'm going out and have a little talk with him. See you later."

René rejoined them at Marc's house, out of breath. "It took some gouging but I got the main lines of it. You were right about Porky. He talked to the older men and women, the ones who would qualify to join, making them swear to keep quiet. He played on that old insurance scandal, said that community action never had and never would be a success in Arsac. He swore that anyone who joined the Co-op would never get goods or credit from him. And, on the other side, people who stuck with him would get a special rebate of ten percent, and when supplies were short they would have a priority. There you have it."

"He's got the whole village bluffed," muttered Marc. "People know Guichard is a cheater. If we could show that they don't have to be dependent upon him, they'd drop him like a dead snake."

Danielle sighed.

"He has won the first round. But our program is clear, to show Arsac people that we are not at his mercy."

René added: "Danielle thought she could show them with a Co-op, which is a logical way, and the way that we must come back to in the end. But there'll have to be a temporary way."

Marc thought a while, and then said, "You must know of Martin Saintain, who has the general store at Margaux, the big one opposite the town hall? He did his military service in the same class as Ovide and Pierre, and more than once I heard my father say that Saintain had had some pretty nasty run-ins with Porky. I'm going to see whether he hasn't some advice for our Committee."

12. *Big Doings*

A T MIDMORN, the Thursday after the sad Sunday of the meeting that did not come off, Hercules Bart, Constable and Town Crier of Arsac-le-Petit, accompanied by sundry children and dogs, and with an occasional rat-a-tat-tat upon his drum, was making his rounds. The public pricked up their ears and stood in doorways. Custom required of him that he pause at eight fixed stations, there beat a double tattoo upon the snare drum suspended from his shoulder, and from a paper in hand read the announcements of that day. As a means of advertising lost animals, turkey shoots, auction sales, and sundry wants and offers, no newspaper could beat Hercules Bart's powerfully voiced proclamations. You needed neither glasses nor education for this kind of advertising, and you'd have to be stone deaf to plead ignorance of the news.

"Rata-tat-tatta, rat-a-tat-tat, tat-tat, *tat*! Hear ye, hear ye! Martin Saintain gives notice that his ambulant grocery will be stationed to the east of the Place de la République, Arsac-le-Petit, between the hours of two to four o'clock on the afternoons of Tuesday, Thursday and Saturday of each and every week. The grocery will carry a full stock of choice comestibles at prices which defy comparison. Fish, dried, smoked and canned; dried fruits, beans, peas and lentils; chocolate and cocoa, coffee and tea; sugar and spices, candles and petroleum, foreign and domestic lard. The ambulant grocery will delight you by its quality and prices. Special feature for today: a beautiful and useful souvenir will be presented, free gratis for nothing, to each lady visitor. Come one, come all. Rat-a-tat-ta-tat-tat."

Jeanne Dufour, on the point of setting out upon the exhausting walk to the distant store, hung up her shopping bag and sat down with a sigh of astonished thanks. At the washing-place, Marisma and Agathe also heard the crier. The smack-smack of wooden paddles upon wet garments ceased. Women with no need to make purchases that day, nevertheless toyed with the thought of artistic and useful souvenirs free gratis for nothing. Monsieur le Curé, extended upon his canvas chair, heard Hercules and nodded, for the food carts to be in circulation was a sign of returning social normalcy. Marc, driving Darnajou's oxen, his now more limber elbow permitting him to grasp a plow handle, leaned against a tree in pure delight. René, sprayer in hand, ran to the edge of the road to hear better. Danielle jumped from the cart to join him.

"That'll give Porky a jolt," said he. "I can hardly wait to see what'll happen."

Porky Guichard also heard. And in all the commune of Arsac he was the only listener who scowled at the news. Saintain was a shrewd salesman. Besides that, a feud had existed between the two men for years. Already Porky was regretting the liberality to which he had committed himself as a means of scotching the Co-op. In fact, he was beginning to cut corners on his discounts. And it did not take him long to realize that an agreement not to join a Co-operative was not the same as a promise not to buy from a rival grocer. If he tried to meet Saintain's prices, and on top of that gave an additional ten percent off, he would lose all his fat profits. No, he did not relish the prospect.

It was a big, roomy trailer, freshly painted, that the Margaux merchant wheeled into the Place. The rear end was wide open, with a counter across, so that customers would look inside. The goods were fresh, with flashy labels. Mr. Saintain would, ordinarily, have sent his son, but today, for the opening, he was there himself, in a white jacket, with flags and flowers stuck about the vehicle to make it festive. He was an experienced hand at jollying village women, full of witticisms which might give offense in other circles, but which provoked vast merriment here, at the edge of the Landes. Also, he knew the value of giving a few grams of overweight, and the rounding off of prices by dropping the centimes. It was service with a smile, a thing which Arsac had not experienced for many moons.

The beautiful and useful souvenirs were celluloid thimbles, which had cost less than a centime, but the lady could choose between pastel blue and pink, and as many remarked, they were feather-light on the finger and easy to find in a work basket.

M. Saintain did not finish waiting on his trade until five o'clock, and left with a shouted farewell promise to persuade his brother-in-law, Antoine, the butcher, to bring his meat cart to Arsac on Saturdays. "Think of it," women nudged one another, "we'll be able to buy beef and mutton right here at home, for Sunday dinner!" It was six years since fresh meat had been sold in their village.

By natural gravitation the Committee of Four was drawn together that evening. They would burst if they did not talk to someone, and it was only safe to talk with one another. Vivette and Danielle strolled up and down the Margaux road until the two boys joined them. "It's marvellous, but how did you ever do it?" Vivette fluttered at Marc. "I went to Porky's this afternoon and you should have seen him. A bear with a sore paw would be angelic beside him."

"You may not believe me," Marc said, "but all it took was to tell Saintain how and why our Co-op meeting went haywire. You see he had a store-on-wheels before the war and he was getting set to resume it. He wanted a special job for his oldest son, and had already bought that trailer. He thinks a lot of Pierre Dufour."

"There's one side of it, just the same, that troubles me," said Danielle. "In getting square with Guichard haven't we slammed the door on having a Co-operative? Saintain will teach people that they are not at the mercy of Porky, but if Saintain establishes a good trade, won't he fill the place that we planned to fill with our Co-op?"

"I saw that objection," Marc explained, "and spoke to Saintain of it, but he made a good point. In a Co-opérative Agricole, groceries are never more than a side line. A Co-op is primarily a farm supply company, dealing with what farmers need for farming, not with what their wives need for cooking. Saintain carries no agricultural stuff."

"So where do we go from here?" René asked.

"We watch from the sidelines, while these grocers fight it out. But by-and-by, say in three or four weeks, when people get used to having two grocery stores, we quietly return to life, and make sentiment for a farm-supply syndicate. Think it over, and see whether that isn't our best bet."

In the end the Committee hewed to that line. They kept their fingers on the pulse of the village but kept their mouths shut, as though the Co-op were a dead issue. Then, in conversations here and there, they began to stress the need for some reliable source of supply for field tools, fertilizer, and wire; fine wire for the vine shoots, medium wire for faggots, standard galvanized wire to support the fruiting branches; nitrate of soda, bone meal, sylvanite, superphosphate; bluestone, sulphur, quicklime in sealed containers; barrel hoops, bonds, disinfecting wicks, bottles and corks; spraying mixtures for fruit trees and potato plants; rope, seed grain, and seed potatoes. Without these essentials, at the appropriate seasons and in sufficient quantities, farming limped and half a man's labor went for nothing, the wine itself coarsened in flavor and shrank in amount.

It was invariably a long-discussed subject and they found plenty of agreement. They sowed the seed of discontent with the present conditions, like underground conspirators.

"We don't need to aim too high," Danielle repeated to the other three. "We only need ten charter members, and we have three right in our own families: Papa Dumartin, Agathe, and my father. Let's pick out twenty people, work on them, and when we think they are converted, write M. Delor to come back. If anyone complains of the three hundred franc fee you can point out that it is only a loan, a deposit to work with, and if the Co-op breaks up they get their three hundred back."

By the end of the month they were able to write M. Delor that they believed that they had seventeen charter members nailed down, and if he could come the following Sunday they would be greatly obliged. They were not advertising the meeting, simply inviting people privately, by word of mouth.

They assembled with the air of lawbreakers, but exulting ones. The widow Houdebaight, whose husband had been a barrel maker, donated as a storeroom the use of his shop which had a wide door and a window opening on the Place. The carpenter loaned a pair of platform scales, "honest scales," he whispered under his breath, and everyone laughed. M. Delor brought a written communication from the Castelnau baker. If the Co-operative would act as a depot for his bread he would sell a three-pound loaf for one franc, fifty centimes less than the regular price. He said it was slow work for his pickup wagon to zigzag among the scattered houses, and he would save that sum in gasoline and driver's wages.

"There is a fourth offer which I will pass over lightly," said the organizer with a knowing wink. "It comes from the United Groceries of Gascogne, the wholesale dealers of Bordeaux. They propose installing a full line of high-grade foodstuffs in the Co-operative's storeroom, without cost to us. Their truck would pass each week to replace what had been sold from the inventory, and to collect for what articles had been sold. They are reliable people and their prices are low. But the grocery situation here in Arsac is somewhat inflamed at the moment. Therefore we had better let this offer lie over for your Committee's later discussion." There were smiles at his caution, but everyone agreed that the grocery problem was too delicate a subject to handle at the outset.

M. Delor's psychology was good. He let the effect of the

favorable offers sink in before he brought out the constitution for their signature, and suggested that they pay their
initiations. Seventeen men and three women signed and
paid.

Now they could get down to the real organizing business,
electing five members for the first Executive Committee.
Some unexpected fun: the way Papa Dumartin after being
nominated for the honor, at first, modestly declined and
then was met by a blast of acclaim from the rest, so that
blushing and overcome, he shrugged his shoulders, nodded,
and submitted to the public will amidst applause.

"Now you won't have to depend on a son-in-law," Pierre
said.

"For that," said Abel Dumartin, "I nominate Pierre Dufour as second member of the Executive Committee!"

Pierre tried with his frantic hands to fend off the cries of
seconding, but he too had to bow to popular demand.

"That puts *you* in your proper place," said Victor.

"So?" said Danielle. "I nominate Victor Esquerre as third
member."

"But neighbors," he protested solemnly, "I am willing to
be helpful in my small way, but since I'm a blacksmith and
the interests of the Agricole, as the very name implies, are
agricultural—"

"That's fortunate," said the barrel maker's widow, who
had donated the storeroom, "it will result in better decisions to have a variety of vocations represented on our
Committee." And as a consequence she too had to accept
a nomination.

From that moment on a comical silence prevailed, everyone afraid of making a suggestion. Finally, Vivette, shaking all over, arose and said in a faint voice, "Monsieur le

Chairman, I would like to nominate the wife of a vineyardist, the wise and good Madame Célestin Labory."

There was round applause both for the choice and for the timid eloquence of Vivette. Mme. Labory, a huge but comely and modest woman, rose and bowed her assent, then sat down again with a tranquil smile as if indulging a throng of children. It was a new, utterly charming gesture in a life-long neighbor, and everybody felt it. Danielle threw her arms around Vivette. "You little imp! What an inspiration for a choice!"

"I'm just still thinking of the household needs and groceries," Vivette answered, pink with her triumph. Others shook hands with the nominees and patted their shoulders in congratulation, for no one would dream of running against them, and each was then unanimously and duly elected.

The new Committee assembled themselves now and sat together. M. Delor, happy as a dancing master with the entire company co-ordinating splendidly, took the floor and gave instructions in how to select goods, to test certain articles and brands for customer-acceptance and preference, how to find out how many of anything to put in stock, and how to control credit. "The general rule, friends, is to be cash on delivery. But limited charge accounts may be advisable. No members, however good a neighbor and skilful a farmer, should receive credit in excess of two thousand francs or be permitted to run a bill longer than ninety days. The object is to help farmers, without favoritism, but to abuse credit is to let a few profit at the expense of others."

That brought applause, and it seemed the meeting was over.

"I seem to be taking a good deal of your time," the organizer continued, "but there is one further item. And it is of major importance—the appointment of our secretary-treasurer. I assume that your storeroom will be open for one fixed hour each day, and for several hours on Saturday and Sunday, as are our other Co-ops. The character of the person in charge of sales and accounts goes far toward making the organization a success. The secretary-treasurer is the single salaried employee of the Co-op, and should be honest, obliging and orderly, above all orderly." He paused and looked around. From both sides of the schoolroom people were smiling at Danielle.

M. Delor caught the hint. "Ah, I see you looking in the direction of Mademoiselle Dufour. Certainly she deserves this recognition. She has our organization at heart. Originally it was her idea. She has the qualifications. She is public-spirited. The usual salary, for beginners, is one hundred francs a month, and she will be under the orders of the Executive Committee."

Another unanimous vote. Danielle was now Secretary-Treasurer of the Co-operative! Never in her wildest day dreams had she thought that such a big, authoritative sounding word would be attached to plain Danielle Dufour.

One more problem came up. How to get the stock from the railroad, over eight kilometers away. If they let the goods pile in the freight yard to make a truck-load, there would be bad delays of urgently needed things; besides, hiring a truck would be too expensive.

Agathe Bracessac arose and offered her donkey. "He's strong, and no more stubborn than some folks we'll have to deal with. And our cart is a pretty good size and solid."

The upshot was that Marc found himself the Co-operative's second paid employee, "the trucker." All this high-sounding committee work, paper signing, and arranging and negotiating, depending on an old indifferent donkey and a clumsy cart, with him holding the reins—the picture was as practical as it was funny.

So everybody laughed and bantered and was serious at the same time.

That evening when Marc and Danielle said goodnight, she remarked: "You know, when I think of this thing we have started, I'm kind of frightened. It seems so *big* all of a sudden."

13. *Dynamite*

ARSAC was still asleep. Danielle had touched a match to the pine cones to heat the coffee and milk for breakfast. She stood in the doorway sniffing the sunrise. The dew was on the grass, the air washed and cool. Dewdrops hung from the serrated points of the vine leaves, golden under the mist. The white scarf of clouds would burn off by ten o'clock and it would be a heavenly day. Since the Co-op had got started she only worked two days a week at Dumartins, and had to be there early. The bluestone adhered longer to the foliage if sprayed before the dew evaporated. She must not dawdle.

The tap-tap of a motorcycle was coming up the road from Bordeaux. The man in the sidecar wore the uniform of an infantry captain. As they reduced speed at the Place de la République, two gendarmes from Macau, who had been keeping out of sight beside the café, wheeled their bicycles toward the Guichard store.

The captain drew a folded paper from his pocket and the younger gendarme gave a smart double knock on Porky's door. There being no sign of life from within, he repeated it. Mme. Guichard's head protruded from the upper window. "Stop that racket," she called; "store doesn't open for two hours yet." She slammed the shutter. But the gendarme, at the captain's nod, kept thumping the door.

This time Guichard himself answered: the sight of a soldier and two gendarmes alarmed him.

"What's the matter?"

"We're here to see you, Monsieur," the captain said. "Come down and open up."

A bathrobe over his night clothes, the merchant came out his door, shut it behind him, and stood, insolently, hands on hips. "Well, here I am. Be quick about it." The man who had driven the motorcycle pushed by Porky, entered the door, looked around until he saw the safe, and sat down beside it.

"I am sorry to wake you so early," the captain said, "but we wanted to be sure to find you at home and that no one had tampered with your accounts. Here is a requisition from the military court of the Eleventh District, authorizing me to remove the records and financial memoranda that may be found in your safe."

Porky was getting set to stage one of his purple-faced scenes of indignation, but the captain held up his hand soothingly. "Save your breath. It will do you no good to anger yourself. If you interfere, the gendarmes are here to lock you up. Be a good fellow, and open the strong box."

"You can't touch my books. I'm a business man. A man has some rights."

The young officer was keeping cool. "I think you'd better

do as I say. If you don't I am instructed to telephone for a truck. We'll carry off the safe and open it at headquarters. And the gendarmes will put you away. So fetch your keys." Porky was waving his fists, but there was fear in his face. His wife, also in hastily covered night-clothes, had descended, and stood beside him.

The captain opened the safe himself, and drew forth from it a sheaf of papers and an account book, which he carried to a nearby desk. His driver pulled up a chair for him, and turned up the wick of the lamp. For a very tense three minutes while the captain looked through these, Guichard stood bowlegged, clenching his fists, a deadly pallor over him. Mme. Guichard was trembling.

"Gendarme," said the captain quietly to the taller of the two, "you will accompany Monsieur to his room, now, and see to it that he gets dressed for a little journey. He will need some shaving articles and so forth."

Guichard actually panted with stupefaction as the gendarme took his arm and marched him out.

"No, no!" Mme. Guichard cried, "Monsieur le Capitaine, no, no, no. Don't take him away!"

"Sergeant," the captain, said unmoved, yet gently, "go back to Macau and telephone for a car." Then turning to the frantic woman, he said, "I'm sorry, Madame, but this will only save time and anguish in case Monsieur should put himself to the terrible experience of trying to run away."

She shrieked and ran upstairs.

The village began to stir, but not until the motorcycle returned did anybody notice that the store had not yet opened. A crowd of inquisitive people gathered, mostly children and women, for the men were already out in the fields. Nobody could make out what it was all about. Maybe

Porky or his wife was very sick? But doctors don't come on motorcycles. No, and it was an army motorcycle. And look, there are two bicycles. What do you suppose? Suddenly an army automobile drew up to the store.

The door of the store opened, and a piercing cry rang out as if someone had been scalded. Two gendarmes emerged, then Porky, in his grey city suit with a gold watchchain and his black derby hat, but pale and breathing through his open mouth. A soldier had him by the arm. There was another cry from within, and out came Mme. Guichard in her night dress, threw her arms around him, and cried out, "My Armand! Don't take my man. He's done no wrong. He's a good man! Armand!"

The gendarmes pulled her away, and Guichard was helped into the back seat of the car, in which the motor was still running; no sooner was the door clapped shut, than the car shot around the Place, and was out of town; the motorcycle with the officer and the other soldier following hard after.

The gendarmes led Mme. Guichard, crying most pitiably, into the store and closed the door behind her.

"What's happened?" everybody asked the gendarmes, who only held their hands outward and declined to say. They pedaled away, leaving behind them the closed store, and the dumbfounded crowd.

"Do you think we ought to go in and speak to her?" one of the women asked the others. They put their hands to their cheeks thoughtfully: Thérèse had been strange, and different ever since her marriage to Guichard. She almost never smiled any more or spoke to anyone sociably, and she had, within the memory of those women standing there, once been a laughing, open-hearted girl.

They ventured to open the door of the store. It was dismal.

"Thérèse!" one of the older women called. "Thérèse?"

No answer. Still as detached from them as ever, Mme. Guichard.

They closed the door quietly and went away.

Nothing was known further about it in Arsac, until, two days later, Marc returning from a Co-op trip to Margaux, brought back a newspaper. Danielle was at the Co-op store, checking over stock, before opening shop for the day.

"Here's the explanation of the mystery of Porky Guichard. He's being held under charges of trading with the enemy." As Marc spoke his face was severe, unexultant.

Danielle took the paper slowly because of this serious expression on him. This was the sort of thing she'd prayed for, that Porky's evil would someday catch up with him, and now that it had she'd almost expected herself to leap, for joy. She'd said she'd have given a lot to be present when he was arrested, and was only sorry that her silly dutifulness of not wishing to play hookey on Papa Dumartin had prevented it. But now only the gravity of the charge against Porky impressed her: treason. She didn't feel much like tossing her cap in the air.

The paper reminded its readers that the foreign invaders had occupied southwestern France with no more than skeleton formations. When these had left in great haste, to everyone's delight, they were so anxious to save their own skins that they abandoned many records and confidential documents. Among these enemy papers, the name of Armand Guichard, Arsac-le-Petit, occurred frequently as a furnisher of cattle, oats, wine, and probably information.

"The rat!" Danielle said, her anger beginning to seethe anew. "While you were endangering your life for our France, he was playing good fellow to the enemy." She looked up at Marc's bad arm.

Marc seemed unimpressed by her anger. He seemed to be thinking seriously of something else. "This newspaper," he said, "if we bring it to Maître Blanchard, right now, before he sees it first by himself, is likely to prove a stick of dynamite that will blow the Dowry Field fraud wide open."

She thought a moment. Blanchard had been in with Porky on that raw deal, and now would have to clear himself of having had dealings with an alleged traitor.

"Marc!" she gasped, "you are right: it is explosive. We must use it while it's fresh. Let's go."

They struck out together, at first walking rapidly, and then slowing up, as arm in arm they laid plans for their surprise attack upon the notary in his stronghold.

They began at once to take full stock of their resources, for you could never tell about a lawyer. And foremost, apart from this newspaper "stick of dynamite" was the fact that since the Co-op had got started and people were buying from the visiting grocer and were no longer dependent upon Porky's grudging service, they began one by one to come to Mathilde and offer to stand witness for her. Not only that, but Agathe and Mathilde had their own bit of evidence. On top of this, Pierre had gone to the Château Cantenac and was told that they certainly would testify that he had been paid by them. That would prove he had the money to pay Porky, though it would not prove that he actually did so. They'd have to depend for that on character witnesses, and Pierre now had a village full of them. Everybody who had had dealings with Pierre Dufour would testify he'd always paid his bills promptly. Then, his good army record!

"Let's not show Blanchard all our case, though," Danielle cautioned.

"No, but let's let him know that we have one," replied Marc.

She looked up and snatched a kiss at the side of his neck, remembering that only a few weeks ago, *he'd* been trying to put up a fight when he'd all but lost morale.

They had themselves pretty well briefed by the time they knocked at the gate in the fence enclosing Maître Blanchard's garden. The notary answered in person. He looked at them with stiff apprehension. Doubtless the arrest of Guichard hadn't benefited Blanchard's morale, Danielle thought, and gave him a cool, measuring smile.

"What do you wish?" he said, clearing his throat.

"To tell you something that may save you some serious trouble, Monsieur," said Marc, stepping inside.

"Mmmh." He turned and walked into the summer-house, pointed out a backless bench for them to sit on, while he took a chair. "Well, what's on your mind?"

"The same thing that's probably on yours," Danielle snapped, so that Marc winced, but it disconcerted the stuffy Blanchard at once: he seemed almost to jerk his chin back as from a boxer's sparring blow.

So Marc quickly followed with, "I suppose it is amply evident to you by now that Pierre Dufour is alive?"

"Mmmh."

"I take it you didn't know he was alive when you drew up the proceedings to deprive him of that piece of land?"

"The war occasions many such errors," the notary said with a shrug. "As for the transference, it was done in strictly legal form."

"No doubt, Maître Blanchard," said Marc. "We know you know the law. However, we know the facts."

"What facts?"

"Facts of Guichard's dishonesty."

"Mmmh."

"Events have yielded us plenty of witnesses," Danielle said, and added sweetly: "It might have occurred to you that our family may not be the only one in Arsac that has been defrauded by Porky Guichard. Doubtless you may have wondered why everybody calls him that?"

The notary was tightening to explode; so Marc turned to her and said, "But Danielle, Maître Blanchard himself is likely totally unaware that Guichard falsified accounts. Do you think that Porky would reveal his crookedness to the notary of Arsac?"

"The accounts M. Guichard showed me," said Blanchard, stiffening up prissily in his chair and arching his eyebrows, "were clear as to the indebtedness of Pierre Dufour."

"Certainly," Marc added in a soothing voice. "But we happen to know that Pierre did have the money to pay Guichard and would and did so before leaving to join the army. We happen to know that Guichard did double-dealing. So he could have one set of books for 'legal' purposes and another for his own memory, and that latter set would have to be accurate. Which set Maître Blanchard saw, or whether he saw both, we don't know, Danielle."

"Only Monsieur's conscience knows," Danielle said slowly as if putting a squeeze on him.

Before Blanchard had a chance to show any reaction to this, Marc drew the newspaper from his pocket, and said, "By now, the military authorities know. Apparently they have all of Guichard's papers. Would you care to read this piece of news, Maître Blanchard?"

The man was pale now. His hand trembled as he tried to adjust his glasses to read. But he managed to summon composure enough to say, "Mmmh."

Danielle and Marc winked to each other to stay silent: make the little old crow do a little cawing now and betray his position.

He folded up the paper and handed it back to Marc, took a comfortable attitude in his chair, and began polishing glasses. "My dear young people," he began suavely, "do you realize what you are doing? Do you know that you are treading on the very edge of libel? And blackmail? Now, I would be very angry with you, but I have known you both all your lives and your families—"

"Precisely, Maître Blanchard," said Danielle, "and that's why we have come here first."

"We could find a capable lawyer through our organization," Marc added, "the Co-opérative Agricole."

"Both that and going to the military authorities and offering them as, as—what's it called, Marc?"

"Friends of the court."

"As friends of the court, we could offer some, oh what's it called?"

"Corroborative evidence," Marc said, as if he'd known that thousand-franc word all his life. "And that, Maître Blanchard, would be rather embarrassing, for without intending libel or blackmail, you see we would be obliged to mention to the officers of the court all the facts and all the names—"

"No, you wouldn't." The notary's trigger-spring little body came into action, he got on his feet. "You wouldn't, simply because I've been intending to go there myself—"

"Why?" Danielle flashed in. "In the interests of your client?"

"Young lady—"

"Why not go in our interests?" Marc now came in, with the trump card. "That's what we came to see you about: to take the case for us. As we said, we could go to a lawyer outside of Arsac, but you have known us all our lives—"

Maître Blanchard looked at them sternly, and then forced a smile upon his face. Perhaps there flowed into it a tinge of admiration. He looked at his watch, and said, "I had intended to be off to Bordeaux by now. I must ask you to excuse me. I must hurry."

He bowed them out by the gate.

Danielle and Marc walked stiffly away, holding apart, until they had got around the turn in the lane, and then flew into each other's arms. Blanchard's slickness had got their Dowry Field away from them; now let him and slickness get it back. He'd have to save himself. Chances were, he was completely guiltless of any treachery to his country, skinflint and hypocrite that he was. So the military court would have nothing on him. If they did they'd have been out here already and got him. But still he'd have to save himself. Save face, but that was all there was to him, face. He'd have to go on living here, and a fraud like that of the Dowry Field along with the bad odor of Porky's trading with the enemy wouldn't be so good for a respected notary, not in Arsac-le-Petit. They'd maneuvered him on to a bad spot of his own making. Now let him get off. They didn't know how he'd do it. But he'd have to.

But as they fairly skipped homeward, they began to realize that maybe they too were on a spot. What about Pierre? How would he take it? After all, the Dowry Field was not theirs yet but his and they hadn't gone to consult him first. They walked more slowly.

They found him hoeing among the vines, and with their

hearts in their mouths they told him all that had happened. He listened, looking pale with anxiety from one to the other, his eyes pleading that the news end up not too disastrous. When they finished, he let out a deep sigh. "Is that all?"

"Yes, Father," Danielle said, taking his hand.

"Well, all I can say is that if it was a foolish thing to do, you did it instead of me. Ever since Jeanne pounced on me for having too long a tongue with Guichard and only making things worse, I've stayed here with a grub hoe holding myself back. So how can I scold you for being like me?"

"Well, don't you think, Pierre, we have the notary in a tight place?" Marc said. "If he's got to clear himself of his crooked client, the Dowry Field might come away clear too."

Pierre shook his head. "I don't know, Marc. One can never know when one entrusts such a matter to a man one has no longer any faith in. And besides, this is only a civil matter. The military court will not be interested."

Danielle and Marc looked at each other dejectedly.

She tried to shrug it off with a smile, as she put her arm around her father. He smiled back, but all three knew that things still looked bad. Blanchard hadn't told them *just what* he was going to Bordeaux for.

14. *Three Women*

Maître Blanchard was not home the next two afternoons when Danielle and her father called. Mme. Blanchard could tell them nothing but that the notary was detained in the city. The Dufours had to make the calls during snatched moments: the busy season was coming head-on for the vineyardists, and the Co-op took every moment of Danielle's time. It left her scarcely thinking space for her own concerns. More than a week had passed when it occurred to her that the Dowry Field was on the far edge of her consciousness and was about to drop out of sight altogether. So after supper she asked her father to see if Blanchard was home.

Pierre found him home all right, rather ingratiating but noncommittal: "Do come in. You look much improved since your return to Arsac," the notary said. "And how is the wife? Aha, aha, aha. No, no, nothing to report yet on the Guichard case, nothing to report. You realize, of course, that the case

the young people have given me, as they think, for they had
no authority from you to do so—"

"Indeed they have: they are acting with my authority,"
said Pierre, bristling.

"Very well, I proceeded under that assumption. But as I
was saying, that case is not exactly watertight," the notary
went on.

"Oh no? Will you oblige me by showing me where the
leak is?" Pierre said, walking up and leaning over the notary's
desk. "Your former client was paid, and he knew he'd been
paid, but he took a chance. He lost. I am now in the position
to have him convicted of one of the meanest, foulest frauds
that a court ever listened to."

"Mmm—" said the notary, leaning back in his chair and
arching his finger tips, "I have here a receipt from your
daughter acknowledging a payment of the surplus of money
which was in excess of the debt."

"There was no debt, I tell you. If a man steals your money
and tosses back a few francs and you take them back, does
that mean he didn't steal? No, Monsieur, whatever the law
might be, it can't be that stupid." Pierre paused for breath.
"Listen, I can get back the field my family has been deprived
of, in two ways. I am— rather *we* are—trying to do so in a
manner that will save delay, expense, and lasting bitterness
in a small community."

"Mmm—?"

"I can instigate a criminal action and win, hands down.
You need little imagination to realize what that will mean
not only to your client, who is now under indictment for
trading with the enemies of France, but what that will mean
also to those who had special dealings with him during that
period."

Pierre Dufour waited for another mmm, but none came. The notary's face froze.

"These parties," Pierre continued, now with less severity, "are doubtless innocent of any treasonable dealings. But contact with a traitor carries a long-lasting odor, Monsieur. To prevent that, to prevent anything so misleading, Maître Blanchard, I prefer the other course of action."

The notary's face relaxed but his eyes were apprehensive as he asked, "Namely?"

"Namely, that through the trusted notary of Arsac-le-Petit the Dowry Field be returned to me certified, taxes paid, free of all leases and encumbrances, in trust for my minor daughter, Danielle, she to receive it upon coming of age or upon marriage."

"Do you know what that entails, M. Dufour?"

"It *should* entail the calling in of certain documents which are false and the drawing up of certain other documents which will be true," Pierre answered, "documents which I should have had drawn up many years ago for safeguarding that property, M. le Notaire, and for which I'll gladly pay you the standard notary fee."

"Mmmm—"

"Good night, Monsieur!"

Pierre stepped out of the gate with a feeling of having been cleansed in soul by a wholesome triumph. He had given Blanchard and the farmer Roger l'Eglise the opportunity to avoid lasting disgrace if they would right a wrong to which they had been accomplices.

The sky had never shone so friendly and full of happy stars for Pierre as it did that night. He walked home with a spring in his step, to tell Jeanne and Danielle.

But when he got there, everybody had gone to bed. These

were days of hard work. He peered into the open door of his daughter's room. The girl was already deep in a well-earned sleep. He put a kiss on her brow, and said under his breath, "Now, my child, you can feel you have a father who knows how to speak for you."

Later on, not much later by the calendar, but years later in terms of events, the Co-operative was occupying the whole ground floor of Mme. Hourdibaight's house, plus the barrel shop, and paying rent for it, the good widow having retired to her upper floor. The small room behind the shop, where the late barrel maker had stored his reserves, was whitewashed and fitted with shelves and counter.

Business at the Co-op was booming. The Executive Committee met each Sunday to vote in new members. They had been bustled into enlargement by the closing of Porky's store, where the windows were shuttered and the door bolted. There now being no place to buy groceries save Saintain's trailer, two hours, thrice a week, the Committee accepted the offer of the Gascogne wholesale company. Old Saintain, feeling he'd got even with Guichard, was glad to retire, and take care of customers elsewhere.

M. Bergeron, a manufacturer from the north and the owner of the Château, gave the young organization a boost by taking out a blanket membership of three thousand francs, in behalf of his personnel, that they might benefit by the low prices. The domain of the Château included a tract of forest, a creamery, a sawmill, brickyard, and charcoal furnaces. This brought in customers quite different from the local farmers—Spaniards, Italians, Arabs from north Africa many of whom spoke little French. Danielle was as pleased as if each new member were doing her a personal favor. The Committee had allowed her to put in a sketchy stock of dressmakers' odds and ends—such things as mothers of families would need to knit, patch, and darn, to remake girls' dresses, and to cut down fathers' trousers for the boys. Marc and Agathe's donkey regularly made a daily trip, sometimes two, to the freight office. Danielle worked twice as many hours as she was paid for. She was accurate and obliging, did not grumble at opening up out-of-hours. M. Delor, who kept an eye upon the infant concern, suggested that the salary of the Secretary-Treasurer be raised, which the Committee did.

After Mass one Sunday noon Jeanne remarked, "Monsieur le Curé is failing. We've been saying that for the last twenty years, so I don't suppose he is, not really. But he does have a fight to breathe."

"I haven't seen him for weeks, I'm ashamed to say," said Danielle.

"The clingstone peaches are ripe. Why don't you pick him a basket? About all he eats is fruit and milk."

Announced by the bell on its circular spring, Danielle came into the shade of the presbytery garden, and shook hands with Father Ambrose, who was sitting in a chair. She handed him the peaches, and seated herself upon the turf at his feet. Within five minutes she found herself talking shop, her shop.

The old priest, as he half reclined in his canvas chair so that he might have but the minimum difficulty in breathing, listened forgetful of his illness and wholly interested.

That was Father Ambrose's wonderful unfreezing quality: speaking few words himself, he irradiated understanding, so that people soon found themselves not only exposing their inner thoughts but unfolding ideas which, they could take an oath on it, had never before occurred in their minds. And this was what was happening now to Danielle.

"Everyone who comes into the store brings a second point of view, I find. To sell him the right things, in the right quantity, and for the price he can pay, I've got to think myself inside of his point of view. Often it's better than mine, especially for him."

Father Ambrose nodded, as if what Danielle was telling him was something that tallied with his own experience.

"Well, Monsieur le Curé, a Spanish woman comes into the Co-op. There must be now about twenty Spanish families, all terribly poor looking. They have fixed up the tumbledown cabins at the edge of the Landes. They do forestry. Well, this woman, she just hangs around and fingers packets of flower seeds with their gaudy pictures, and the bright patterned cottons. I feel an ache inside, the way she can't bear to let pretty colored things out of her hand, but she is holding only one coin, and that must go for bread."

Danielle paused and her eyes fell on the basket of peaches. Why was she telling all this? She had come merely to bring Father Ambrose these peaches. But she had started some thinking aloud which she couldn't stop.

"I wish you could see her, Monsieur le Curé: with one baby straddling her hip, and another peeking around her skirt." Danielle was up on her feet imitating the woman. "The baby is pale and thin, but she has nothing to give it but bread and potato soup. And, and I can't help thinking how awful it is to watch a baby fade away and not be able to do anything to save it."

The rustle of the old man's asthmatic breathing became more audible, but he lifted a hand to stay his young visitor. He closed his eyes as if to sink back into a deep sleep. His breathing became less and less effortful. In a few moments he opened his eyes with a smile, and said quietly, "Yes, Danielle, we were putting ourselves in this mother's place."

Danielle's spinning mind had momentarily lost the image of the Spanish mother. She prepared to leave. "I'm afraid, Father, I'm not so good for you, with this excitement."

"You are very good for me, my child. Be seated. Let us return to our subject. There are many children in Arsac who do not have enough to eat."

"I know, because I see what people buy. . . what little they can afford. And here I thought our Co-operative was going to be a miracle."

"A miracle is not always at first obvious."

"I wish we could give them something besides pins and buttons and groceries at the Co-op. That's not enough. Those Spanish women need a doctor, but their husbands can't make enough to afford one. If only our Co-op could sell her, oh, you know, Monsieur le Curé, the really good things: the pleasure, the beauty, that she has a right to, the health of her babies, and not have it always cost money."

A bell seemed to ring within Danielle. She sat bolt upright, looking through the foliage at the vision that came then into her mind. "A co-operative health center for infants! Why should our co-operation stop anywhere?"

"If le bon Dieu has given you that idea, my child, He has given you a responsibility. In the village your Co-operative and Church are the only two places where people meet with the constant purpose to assist one another." He lay back and thought a moment. "Would you feel less alone in this venture, Danielle, with a somewhat older woman for a working partner? A woman of education, say, and practical experience?"

"Oh, yes!"

The next afternoon Danielle returned to the Curé's garden, full of curiosity but somewhat subdued by her down-to-earth Marc. He said she must be suffering from excessive exposure to the sun to want to sell the bred in-the-bone individualists that made up the Executive Committee such a starry-eyed idea.

In the Curé's garden, she met and recognized a young woman in black, Diane Lescure, the middle daughter of M. Bergeron of the Château. It was Diane's sisters that Mathilde washed for. Diane had married and lived elsewhere during the war. But she had recently lost her husband and returned to the peace of the country. Her face had much sweetness emerging from a look of having suffered great anguish.

"I enjoy having you two girls meet," said the priest, placing Danielle's hand within that of Mme. Lescure. "You have both come to me and talked in much the same vein."

Mme. Lescure's soft, small hand had a warm grasp. She had driven an ambulance during the hostilities and been a nurse's aid, the Curé said, and then he told her something about Danielle. He described one to the other back and forth in a quaint, playful way, and soon had them laughing lightly. Danielle had too much to do and Diane had been deprived of anything to do, since her bereavement.

"I can't stop thinking, thinking, thinking, until it seems I will go insane," the lady confessed.

"I know just how that is," Danielle said. "For a while I just chewed on myself like a trapped animal. But, thank God, it was necessary for me to work—"

"It is also necessary for Diane," said the priest, "for her peace of mind."

Soon they were into the subject of the health center.

"In the same house with our store, Mme. Hourdebaight has a big airy parlor. Whitewashed, it would be absolutely the thing for a dispensary. I feel sure she would rent it to us," said Danielle.

Diane's eyes were sparkling now. "How would it be if I tried to persuade the doctor at Margaux to donate his services for an hour a week, until the members' subscriptions begin coming in? There is enough unused furniture in the Château garret: chairs, a big table, cabinets for the medicines and the cans of powdered milk. Why, I can see it all already. The women would bring their babies in each week, for a checkup. The doctor would prescribe calcium for their bones, and so on, where necessary. We could help women get what is indispensable, the Co-op paying part, and in critical cases, paying all. I know how to get in touch with the child-help societies. Besides, I have been a nurse. My father is himself a hard worker, and he'd love to have a hand in this. Getting people back on their feet has become his main interest in his business. I'm sure he'll pay the rent."

What Diane was proposing outran Danielle's fondest expectations. Her cheeks lit up with red tinges of excitement. "Think what it will mean. Here in Arsac we never get a doctor until it is too late. So, many women go around sick with worry because their babies are ailing. And some have to work in the fields all day. Heaven knows what they do with the tiny ones then."

The priest and Diane exchanged glances.

"My dear," said Diane, "only three days ago I came across a woman who is doing that very thing: watching over the little ones, and in her own crude way doing a bit of nursing among the sicklings. It was my interest in working with her that brought me to Father Ambrose, and then to you. I'd like to have you meet her."

"Where is she?" Danielle asked quickly. "Women like that are the kind I'd like to know."

In another minute the two young women had taken their leave of Father Ambrose and received his blessing. They walked out of the village at a brisk pace and chatted just as rapidly. Mme. Lescure asked many questions about Danielle's wartime peregrinations, and rewarded the ready replies with generous accounts of herself, which Danielle hesitated to ask about but was eager to know. This little wisp of a lady with melancholy rings under her eyes had seen harsh duty under fire, but she seemed to accord Danielle's experience the same respect she received from her.

They came to a small cottage at the far edge of the village. It had been empty the last time Danielle had seen it, before the war. She tried to remember who used to live in it.

With the recollection came the fact that stunned her: here, years ago, had lived the grandmother of Thérèse Guichard! And there opening the door was Mme. Guichard herself.

Danielle's blood turned to ice. She looked at Mme. Lescure as at a betrayer. All at once the charming lady with her smile became something alien, sinister.

Mme. Guichard bowed meekly to them both. "Please come in, Madame and Mademoiselle," she said motioning to some chairs. She was carrying an infant in one arm and another was crawling on the floor. Her face was gaunt and her eyes bloodshot. Not looking directly at Danielle, she seemed to sway and grope for a chair.

Mme. Lescure darted over and helped her to sit down. "I have given both of you a shocking surprise," she said, relieving the older woman of the child, a three-month old puny, hairless thing that looked more like an unsuccessfully made rag doll than a real human baby.

"I'm afraid so, Madame Lescure," said Porky's wife, her forearms shaking in her lap.

Danielle could not pry open her own rigid lips to utter a word.

"If you will forgive me for moralizing," Mme. Lescure said, "most wonderful things are born in great pain." She closed her elegant little hand over the infant's bare foot, and sat down. "In this room I have before me the two women out of all the people in Arsac who can save these helpless children from a dreadful start in life. Do you think it would be fair to these babies if I neglected to bring you together?"

Porky's wife looked at her with clenched fists and an amazed stare, and Danielle turned away, feeling an impulse to dash out of the door. Was Mme. Lescure crazy? Did she perhaps have some unbalance of mind from her war experiences? Didn't she realize that the Guichards were crooks, misers, despicable beyond any decent person's tolerance? It gave Danielle gooseflesh merely to think of any association with Porky's wife.

But Mme. Lescure's soft voice went on: "If we had a million francs for our health center and did not have what is within you two women, it would fail."

She described the sketchy plans to Mme. Guichard, and said if the health center did at all well it would be too much work for fewer than three women, two to be on duty and one off. As she spoke she fondled the wretched infant casually as if it were her own.

The other baby, about a year old, was an olive-faced, dark-eyed boy, rather pretty as he watched the women, in wondering silence and in need of a nose-wiping. Mme. Guichard lifted him to her lap with a smile that Danielle had never seen before on her, and it seemed that the woman in doing this was taking refuge from the situation and Mme. Lescure's incredible idea.

"Mme. Guichard has told me that since her husband has been held by the military court, their establishment has been padlocked by the court, and she had nowhere else to go but here, in her grandmother's house. Nobody has visited her. She was in somewhat the same situation as I, desolately idle. So she took to visiting the foresters' cabins and looking after the little ones of the Spanish and other families."

No! No! A million times, No! said Danielle's mind. If we let that woman get a toe-hold in our dispensary she'll ruin it. Half the trouble in this town is due to her husband. Every decent person will quit us, if she's connected with it.

Mme. Lescure touched the infant's chin with her little finger and made it smile. You'd think that the pallid creature were a cherub with a heavenly aura, to see the lady's delight over this.

"Here, my dear," she said, getting up, and placing the baby in Danielle's half-willing arms. "This will tether you; isn't that so, Mme. Guichard?"

Porky's wife was forced to reply. "I am in deep disgrace in Arsac," she said, turning her face aside. "I can expect no consideration from Mlle. Dufour."

Danielle said nothing. The small weight in her arms moved and she hoped the baby wouldn't cry.

"We are three childless women," said Diane Lescure.

"Mlle. Dufour, you at least can look forward to having your own. Mme. Guichard and I cannot. I don't think I am misusing her confidence when I tell you what she told me?"

Mme. Guichard shook her head. "I can have no comfort in maintaining my secrecy," she said, while a tear rolled down her cheek.

Diane Lescure went over and stood behind her chair, putting a hand on her shoulder. "Mme. Guichard has told me that her childlessness was so deep a disappointment that it pained her to associate with women who had children. So she devoted herself to—to narrow interests."

"I was very greedy," Porky's wife said, looking down at the ground. "If my husband did wrong I didn't know what it was. But it was my fault. I encouraged him to make all the money possible, because I felt that the people of Arsac didn't like us. They seemed to look down on us from their happiness with their children playing and singing and laughing in their houses. The morning the military came and took my husband from me and left me alone with all the store shut around me, the property my greed had gathered, I knew it was all worthless."

She spoke in an even, hard tone, as if she thought any gentleness in it would appear to be self-pity. Instead, she gave the gentleness to the baby boy on her knee. She bounced and patted him as she spoke.

"So I went over to Monsieur le Curé for confession. My penance is going on right now, to bow to those whom I have wronged."

Danielle couldn't look at her, but stepped over to the window with the baby and looked outside. It no longer seemed like a trick played on her, but she didn't like it. Did they think she had no self-respect? Here she was deprived of her dowry by this very woman and now was she expected to kiss and make up? As for the health center, there were people in Arsac who were going to think it absurd enough without the spectacle of Pierre's daughter and Porky's wife working together in it.

She opened her lips to say something, but stopped because all she could think of was resentment and hatred. Oh, if Marc were only here with her!

"This is the most dismaying difficulty we'll have to over-come in our entire work," Diane Lescure said, "what both of you are going through this minute."

"I know everybody in Arsac hates my husband, and me. They call him 'Porky,' and they should call me 'Sow,' by the same justice. He will be sorely punished and I may never again see him. But however they blacken him, I want Ar-sac to know he wasn't a bad man. He was a spoiled man. Ask the oldtimers. They'll tell you he was left here, an abandoned orphan, during the big war before this last one. But only Father Ambrose will tell you what persecution he endured because he was so melancholy-looking and an outsider, as he grew up here under my grandmother's care. I too was homely. No other boy would look at me. So we married. There, Danielle Dufour, you now have my soul at your feet," she said, scarcely above a whisper, looking up at the younger woman and then down on the floor. "You may step on it, spit on it, if you wish. I can only give thanks to Mme. Lescure for bringing you here to let me offer myself to you for humiliation."

Thérèse Guichard was now weeping gently into one hand.

Mme. Lescure took the child from her, and then brought her a glass of water. "Now, my dear, take heart," she said.

"We are down to the floor, as far as we can go. We can only step upward from here on."

She kissed the woman's brow, set the baby down, and started to leave.

There was nothing for Danielle to do but to place the infant she held in Thérèse Guichard's arms. As she did so, she looked her straight in the eyes, which was the most she could do. She couldn't say anything to her at all.

As they stepped outside, Danielle noticed that the long-neglected geraniums in the dooryard had been trimmed and had a vivid tint. All around were signs of recent careful mulching and cultivating. She fought off all the meanings these signs had that Thérèse Guichard had grace in her.

Diane Lescure took Danielle's arm as they walked slowly away. "She has sold her personal things, like trinkets and furniture, to buy food for herself and for the Spanish children. I found her making clothes for them. By herself, mind you! She seems to be an excellent dressmaker, and has sewed some perfectly cunning dresses for the little girls."

Danielle shook her head. "I cannot tell you anything now, Madame Lescure," she said. "Things have come too suddenly and too thick at me. You must give me time."

She took her leave and turned homeward.

It seemed that whenever something good happened, like getting this wonderful idea for a health center, and you were sky-high in delight over it, something else had to come along and interfere.

She made toward her Trouble Tree to think it out, but now all of a sudden that struck her as a childish thing to do: this was too difficult even for the cherry tree to be much help. Go to Father Ambrose? But she knew what he'd say.

His teachings sounded beautiful, and you'd feel that you

could go right out and do everything noble. But when it came to an actuality like this, it wasn't so easy.

Then she imagined herself telling all this to Marc. And a strange thing occurred within her thoughts: she found herself putting up the arguments to him that Mme. Lescure might have put up to her! "Thérèse Guichard sits up all night with a sick baby so that its mother can get enough sleep to work in the vineyards the next day. And the vineyards are the bread-and-butter for all of us. What kind of Co-op secretary would I be, just because of my private grudge, or yours, or anybody's to stop her? No, Marco, that doesn't add up right in my kind of bookkeeping."

Then she imagined what her mother would say. Jeanne would snap: "No. It's impossible. I can't let it be. It rubs me wrong, my fur doesn't grow that way." And the next night you'd find her working right alongside of Thérèse Guichard trying to save the life of a baby with the croup.

Danielle smiled to herself over this thought. Her decision was made.

She decided to tell Marc first of anybody. That evening, after the Co-op was closed, they sauntered among the vineyards encircling the village. Marc and she were commenting upon what each owner had done or left undone, judging each man severely by his work. This was customary. They had in childhood overheard their fathers converse like this with their mothers during evening strolls home from church. The only difference was that she and Marc were all the time observing, learning, noting the mistakes which they must not make. And by now Danielle had been so well coached by Papa Dumartin in the culture of the vine that Marc knew he was speaking with his peer in that knowledge. And he liked it. It tickled him to hear Danielle pop up with some fact of viniculture usually known only to the menfolk, and the experts at that. "Now, tell me, Danielle," he'd exclaim, "where'd you get that?"

It was at a time like this that she told Marc the whole story of meeting Mme. Lescure and discovering Mme. Guichard. Then her decision.

He looked at her amazed, incredulous.

"What's the matter, Marco?" she asked, tremulous, but tenderly, for she knew just what kind of shock he was getting. "Don't you approve? Won't you stand by me?"

"I'll stand by you in anything, you know that."

"Then you don't approve?"

"Approve? How can I approve something so entirely outside of my way of thinking?"

"If you disagree, Marc, I'm half beaten."

"No, I don't mean that. I mean it's outside of my understanding. All this time I've felt I've known you so well, and I've been saying to myself, there's no mystery to women. Danielle is as clear as daylight to me. And now you spring this on me, and frankly, I confess I'm mystified. You women are mysterious, surely enough!"

"Suits me!" she laughed and blew at his curls.

15. *"Throw In Your Grapes!"*

WITH the yellowing of the leaves a certain breathlessness descended again upon this vineyard country as it had in the days before the war. Young and old felt the tension. For fifty weeks, as the oldtimers of Arsac would reflect, the whole family slaves for the grape roots. Then for two weeks, if the capricious vines be gracious, they pay back a little. But for fifty weeks they are insatiable. A man might beggar his children to feed his vines, wear down himself, his wife, and his cattle to pamper his vines,

and still fall short of satisfying them. Now the time had come around when he would find out. Now he'd see if he had a crop or a defeat.

There was nothing more you could do to improve the crop. You had done everything, and the rest was a gamble. You could only stand by and wait and watch. A frost might strike too early. A day-long fog might mildew the stems. Or, by Heaven's favor, dew and light showers might drench the plants by night to swell the fruit into luxurious size, and the sun by noon come hot so as to fill the juice with sugar.

But there was much to do to be prepared for good luck. From sunrise to sunset there was the bustle among the winemaking equipment that the Dufours and many another citizen of Arsac hadn't seen in years. Thumping of empty barrels to make them tight, the burning of sulphur within them to sterilize them, the scrubbing of cavernous vats, the sweeping of cobwebs from dim rafters. Clippers being sharpened and oiled, wagon wheels greased, wooden baskets stacked conveniently outside doorways, copper soupcauldrons polished to a sheen.

Everybody was glad to have this work to take the mind off the anxiety of a crop failure.

Danielle was having more than her share of activity, for the Health Center was now a fact. In the widow Hourdebaight's parlor, mothers from the farthest edges of Arsac were presenting their babes for Dr. Amannieux to poke and peer at under his shaggy brows. Danielle busy in the store could hear on the other side of the wall the muffled squealings and yippings, and it was all sweet to her ears.

In fact, she wished she could leave her shopkeeping and be in the next room with Vivette, who in a white dress, with her bright blonde hair and tinkling laugh could stop a baby from crying. Vivette was showing talent for nursing, and the doctor was so charmed by her and impressed with her neat, deft ways, that he had her bicycling in to town to learn more at his office. The boxes and cans and implements of the shop looked prosaic to Danielle, in comparison to Vivette's work.

The doctor's weekly verdict and his telling the mothers what to do were not enough, though. It was another job to get the mothers to do it. Many of them scarcely understood French and some not at all. They had migrated here bringing nothing but what they could carry in their two hands. Their wages supplied food but that was all. They couldn't furnish homes with what they earned. They washed themselves, their crockery, their garments, in the same brook they took their drinking water from. They lived in almost a stone-age primitiveness.

To see that the doctor's recommendations were carried out required a visiting nurse. The success of the Dispensary depended upon her. And Arsac had two, Diane Lescure and

Thérèse Guichard. Diane, in her Red Cross uniform, made her rounds by pony cart and on foot. Thérèse went about quietly, sitting up all night to aid the arrival of infants. Unless an Arsac woman needed her, none ever saw her, except at Mass. There was at first a little whispering and nudging, but soon one by one people greeted her. She would return the greeting and continue on her way. It seemed odd behavior for Porky's wife to be so charitable, but she had always been retiring, and indeed she became so much like the long forgotten Thérèse Moreau, that everybody was soon enough accustomed to her. Danielle breathed easier.

But another anxiety arose. The Health Center was growing faster than its funds. The Co-op couldn't support itself and the Center too. "It's like two people drowning together," Danielle said, "because one of them can't swim."

Donations, further help from M. Bergeron were out of the question. "We're a Co-operative, not an endowed charity outfit," Marc said.

"I can't bear the idea of people coming up to us crying, 'I told you so!' And there are a few only too ready to do it," Vivette sighed, as she looked over her spotless white dispensary.

"And the season coming along so beautifully," Danielle said, gazing out of the window. Even the weather had a special pre-vintage note. Goldenrod and Michaelmas daisies were taking on a definite outline. At noon, she had noticed the wasps and bumblebees at their noisy foraging, guzzling over-ripe grapes which had burst their skins. And at sunrise, she remembered, a grey gossamer of moisture lay upon the land. The foliage was ethereal, the trees like trembling specters, the neighbor's barn and house diaphanous, so that she'd felt the world she'd wakened to was still part of her dreams. In the hollows and dells, lakes and islands of fog had settled, and she'd noticed the scarves of the fairytale "white ladies" bowing out into invisibility as the sun rose hand-high.

"Dreaming Danielle," said René Dumartin.

"Just think," she answered, "it will be the first real vintage for three years."

"The first in four or even five years, for those who have been prisoners or in the army," René added.

"Some of the big owners who had the capital to pay wartime prices, for supplies and labor," Marc said, "those are the ones who will have a good crop, maybe. So will a few forehanded peasants like your family, René."

"Yes, I guess we are the fortunate ones," said René, his eyes following every motion of Vivette's hands stitching mouth-masks.

"Most of us here in Arsac, though, are little people," Danielle said, still looking out of the window, "one-man farms, like us Dufours, and with the man away what happened? The vines just lay down and quit. It's a pity this first vintage can't be a nice one for all of us."

The anxiety for the harvest dwelt on everybody like another kind of mist, she thought, one that hung around all day with foreboding.

"Yes, guess it can't be helped," Marc chanted resignedly where he sat on the patients' waiting-bench. "Those who haven't any crop will turn sour, and tell their young ones about the good old days when every family had a fat pig for Christmas and a dozen hens or so for Sunday stews. I get tired of such talk." He yawned, and swung his right arm slowly over his lap. It was getting better. He could almost pull a box off the cart with it now. "You can't eat the past."

"Just the same I'd like to see everybody this year full of beef soup and rejoicing at vintage," said René.

"That's what I say," Vivette put in. "You gloom sprayers, you've almost got me thinking this dispensary's going to close up."

"Pretty near to it, right now," Marc said. "But don't call me a gloom sprayer or I'll bite those dimples out of you."

"Say," Danielle said, coming away from the window and rubbing her head, as if she were about to faint. "I've an idea."

"Mon Dieu!" Marc collapsed on the bench. "Another Danielle idea!"

"Listen, this is something that's going to work out for rich and poor alike. And if it's the Co-op that works it—"

"The Co-op?" Marc shouted. "We're worked to a frazzle as it is. All night it goes on in my sleep: 'co-op-co-op-co-op' like a frog. And look at her, will you! It's aging her already."

"Marc!" Vivette screamed. She had been doing Danielle's hair in a new way and was proud of the effect. "How can you say that? Danielle's lovely."

"Yes, I swoon at the sight of her. But mostly because I'm too tired to hold my eyes open. And she's so tired every night I hardly see her. What kind of life's that?"

"All right, I'm about to die, then," Danielle said. "But listen to my dying words. You know that the big properties around here recruit bands of pickers in the cities. They have to, ordinarily, because then all the local folks would be working for themselves. But this year the little people haven't any grapes."

"You think they'll work on the big properties?" René said. "No, they're too stiff-necked independent."

"Only about asking for jobs," Danielle retorted. "I know, because I've been one of them. So the big growers'll just do as always: bring in the outsiders, paying transportation, lodging, and food, besides fees to their foreman. Why can't the Arsac people get that good food and the high pay? Why can't we organize troupes of our home people?"

"Too much *work!*" Marc shouted. "All your ideas are nothing but work."

"That's why they succeed, Marc," she answered. "All hands will gain. The proprietors save transportation, lodging, foreman's pay."

"What does the Co-op get out of it though?" Vivette was wailing now. "And our poor little dispensary."

"Gracious! The vintage money!" Danielle cried. "It stays in Arsac. And where in Arsac can you spend a franc but at the Co-op?"

"The lady has a grand point!" René came in. "Pickers are going to get a hundred francs a day. Carriers and pressworkers a hundred-and-fifty."

"Best of all," Danielle added, "it will be a *community* vintage!"

Marc sighed. "I'm afraid it'll be a success. I'm against it. How'll I ever get any sleep?"

"If you want to be an old bear, Marc Bracessac," said Vivette, "you can sleep all winter."

As Marc feared, it worked.

"This is one of those things so excessively simple," M. Dumartin told the Executive Committee, "that you kick yourself because no one thought of it before."

And also, as Marc had feared, the work was enormous. Merely the preparatory part of it: scouting around to organize working-groups and guaranteeing that the big growers would have them, and then hardest of all, getting and laying in stock at the Co-op in anticipation of the boom.

He and Danielle walked home from the Co-op so tired at night they could hardly speak to each other. Even during her wanderings she'd never been so weary.

Marc wasn't really a grumbler, but both he and she knew he was becoming grumpy. He was a believer in moderation. And now in his fatigue he felt that this girl of his was at heart a radical and given to excesses. And he told her so.

"Is this the way it's going to be always?" he asked. "What kind of home life will it be for us?"

She was too tired to answer, let alone argue. All she knew was that a need had called her, and she had given herself to it. But was she risking Marc? After all, a home, a man has a right . . .

The rush season approached nearer and nearer. Eleven growers among the Co-op members at once contracted for the work-groups, and seven among the non-members. Going around on Vivette's bicycle, Danielle tried to assign pickers to properties that were near their homes, and to be sure that she didn't get people with long-standing feuds into the same group: men quarreling through the decades over a boundary fence, sisters-in-law who hadn't spoken for twenty years. Arsac had its share of that sort of thing.

One day Marc returning from the freight station brought back a paper with him. Armand Guichard's trial. And his sentence. The outcome probably wouldn't please any of his bitter enemies in Arsac. It had been proved that he was a purveyor of grain, meat, and wine to the occupation forces. He had cornered canned meat and precious flour, forcing his country to pay unheard of prices. In the social gatherings of the enemy officers he had been a hale-fellow-well-met. But it had not been proved he was an informer. His was a borderline case —not bad enough for penal servitude but too serious to be acquitted. The Court, therefore, pronounced a sentence that was being applied in many similar cases: confiscation of property and loss of citizenship for ten years. His real estate was to be sold at auction, his bank accounts and other assets seized, for remedy or restoration of any loss suffered by his fellow townsmen through any misdealings, of which there had been notably one, as represented by his own former notary of Arsac-le-Petit.

That evening Maître Blanchard called at the Dufour cottage and placed papers in Pierre's hands.

"When you have carefully examined these, Monsieur Dufour," the notary said briskly, "you will conclude that you are in possession of a clear title and deed to the whole of your property. In fact, you will find that the legal status of it is better than formerly."

"It couldn't be better," Pierre blazed. "The Dufours have owned that since—"

"You will find the entire history in those papers. Tomorrow, if you are satisfied, you will do me the honor of coming to my house to have your signature witnessed. My compliments, Monsieur, and good evening."

The papers were sound as a wagon spoke. The next evening, Pierre brought Papa Dumartin with him to witness the signature.

"To think," he said, when he came home, "that all this

was unnecessary but for a dishonest man."

Danielle and Marc were glad they had the Dowry Field back, but not so glad as they'd wish to be. They were too tired. They did not even have the time to go out and look at it.

But neither Guichard's sentence, nor the return of the Dowry Field was big news in Arsac. The big news was that the harvest of grapes was to be a beauty! Perfect. People became doubly busy as the vintage rolled forward according to schedule. Early to bed, well fed, laughing much, fingers and lips purple from grape juice. The Co-op's bands of pickers and pressmen were everywhere pleasing to the big growers. They were steadier than city folk, many of whom only came for a lark.

Up and down the alleys of vines, the carriers went with their yawning baskets, adjuring the pickers: "Messieurs, Madames, throw in your grapes! Throw in your grapes!"

Jeannot picked at Dumartin's. Pierre carried a basket at The Hillock. Jeanne exercised her talent as a soup-maker at Monbrison. Mathilde did the same at the Château, where M. Bergeron's small army consumed loads of bread and roast sheep daily.

In the midst of all this activity Guichard returned.

It was a subdued man who came home, and he returned to Arsac because there was nowhere else for him to go. Gone were his bounce, his aggressiveness. His gimlet eyes which used to bore through you, now were turned down. A dead silence fell around him as he walked among the villagers.

In a measure, Thérèse had softened animosities, but the feeling against him was everywhere evident. Men whom he had believed to be his friends only shook their heads and tightened their mouths when he asked them for a loan. They wanted no dealing with a formerly suspected traitor.

Early risers caught a glimpse of him, pedaling off on a ramshackle bicycle: a box of needles, thread, shoelaces, buttons, pencils, and hairpins strapped to the handlebars. He had not the face to be a peddler in the village where he until lately had been a top man. But even where he went, at distances, his bad reputation had gone before him. People set the dog on him. At length, at the bottom of the scale, he found a job wheeling sand for a road mender.

But Arsac was not subdued. Vivette and several other girls thought the Community Vintage should be celebrated with a gala party. Mme. Lescure warmed to the idea. She would get the electrician from Margaux to string colored bulbs from the pressroom ceiling. They would revive some of the oldtime customs, such as having the prettiest girl in each troupe ride in on the last wagonload of grapes, with a bouquet for the owner. As if Arsac did not already have its fill of committees and doings, Blanche the blacksmith's wife was put in charge of decorations; Marisma, whose gingerbread was famous, in charge of refreshments; René, in charge of the music.

Vivette herself was too busy at the Health Center and the Co-op. Danielle and Marc liked the idea, but were listless.

In the midst of all this the government decided to hold the auction of Guichard's store. The Executive Committee decided that there was nothing else thinkable but to buy it, if the bidding did not exceed the funds they could hurriedly muster.

When the hour arrived, the only outside bidder was Martin Saintain, the grocer from Margaux. His bid was so low that everybody's jaw fell. The auctioneer said, "I beg your pardon?"

Saintain repeated the bid.

"Do I hear another?" the auctioneer looked around.

Papa Dumartin then softly spoke the bid of the Co-opérative Agricole of Arsac-le-Petit. The auctioneer blenched, though it was a considerable advance over the previous bid.

He looked around, called in vain for further bids. He frowned, and orated about the merits of the property. Finally, he threw his hands up, and said in a dejected voice, "Sold."

A great shout of hearty laughter rose from Martin Saintain. He strode over to Papa Dumartin, shook his hand and slid into his car. With a wave of his hand to the people of Arsac he drove off.

Danielle knew he was trying to get the last drop of vengeance out of his late competitor. But should good come out of such a bad motive? Good it certainly was for the Co-op to have the larger quarters of Guichard's store.

As she watched the Committee pay the auction officials, she knew that if two months ago anybody had predicted this she would have danced for joy. But she felt strangely unexultant. The auctioneer party left, and Papa sat back in his chair.

"Well, friends, the Co-operative has become a full-sized establishment, and there is no one more to thank for this than Mademoiselle," and he bowed smilingly toward Danielle, "this girl of Pierre's," nodding to her father. Pierre returned the nod gravely. He didn't seem elated either.

This was the first time in her life she had heard "girl of Pierre's" and not quite enjoyed it. Out in the vineyards, among the pickers and carriers she'd heard it: "Well, if here isn't Pierre's girl!" and now and then a grower would say to her upon approach, "And so you are that girl of Pierre's? You've certainly grown."

The Committee members, except her father, were watching her, to see what she would say.

Somewhere outside two shots rang out very loud. And near. People looked at one another.

"That's a shotgun," said Victor slowly, and everybody got up to look outside.

People were running toward the Guichard store. She heard somebody cry, "Porky." And then somebody else said. "No, I saw Marc run back there."

Quick as a flash, Danielle ran around the back of the store. There Marc was standing, his hands on his hips facing Porky Guichard, who was sitting on a box with his face buried in his hands—and of all people, Jeannot, panting like a terrier.

"Why, why did you stop me?" Porky was sobbing hoarsely. "Why don't you let me leave a life not even a worm would want to live?"

In another moment people from all over had gathered around to gaze upon the man hiding his face in his hands. He evidently didn't hear or see them. "Today, after but one day's trial, I lose my job wheeling gravel. Now I can't even make a success of killing myself."

Danielle ran around to the well, where somebody had left a filled pitcher. She came back.

"Here," she said to him, and her voice in spite of her intention was a little rough and not quite kind, "you better drink a little water."

He let the pitcher be brought to his lips, and then discovered the crowd of his townsmen silently watching him.

Again he covered his face with his hands. Danielle took her handkerchief, moistened it with the water, and sponged his forehead. He was a man who had expected to be dead, she thought, and it was as though he had lost the feel of being alive.

She looked behind her and noticed that Pierre and Papa Dumartin were gently herding the people away.

Father Ambrose appeared suddenly. He bent down and put his arm over Porky's shoulders.

"Come, Armand," he said sternly, "come with me."

The broken man, still hiding his face in his hands, allowed himself to be guided by the old priest across the Place.

At a distance the crowd followed to the Curé's garden and watched the pair disappear in the gate.

Low-toned and whispered enquiries and comments were going on everywhere.

"Marc saved his life," Jeannot was saying, still panting. "Marc's a hero."

"No, it wasn't me. It was Jeannot," Marc said.

The effects of it were just beginning to hit Danielle. Her knees seemed to give way.

Marc and Pierre took her by the arms.

"You might have been killed," she said.

"No, not with Marc," Jeannot said. "He got his arm under Porky's chin and dug one knee into his back, so Porky had to drop the gun."

"Then Jeannot climbed up on him in front and hung on to him while I fired both barrels," Marc said, chuckling. "It was he who told me. He came running up to me where I was sweeping out the cart. 'Hey, Marc,' he says, 'I just saw Porky sneak around back of the store with a shotgun!'"

"How'd you see him, little one?" Pierre asked. "Aren't you

supposed to be working out at Dumartin's?"

The boy's attention was attracted to Bernalac's spaniel, but he managed a reply while teasing the dog:

"Well, Monsieur Dumartin brought me in with him so I wouldn't miss the auction, and after it was over, I was poking around back over there looking for stuff and I saw Porky come sneaking around in back of the houses with a gun, and I thought it looked funny to be out hunting this time of the day."

The spaniel took off to join some other dogs and boys, and Jeannot followed. The incident was closed for him.

The small crowd smiled a little relieved, and stood waiting outside the Curé's gate without asking themselves why. Papa Dumartin and Célestine Labory, however, went back to the Co-op, and a few others began slowly drawing away.

"Wonder what he's telling him?" Mme. Hourdebaight said.

Who telling whom? Danielle wondered. But fat Felix Dassier, who had lent her his horse for plowing, answered with a twinkle: "Monsieur le Curé does his best preaching in his garden." Father Ambrose wouldn't preach to a man in Porky's condition. But maybe Felix didn't mean preaching, exactly: it was just his simple idea of the Curé's kind way of speaking, when every word cost him a toilsome breath. Anyhow, thought Danielle, looking about her, everybody there seemed to understand Felix and agree with him: everybody there evidently had been at one time or other in the Curé's garden alone with him, with some anxiety or woe. But none like this: a man returning to life, to Arsac to live. She saw standing around her those who, like herself, had been away and returned to Arsac—all had come back in bad condition. None, though, so bad as Porky. But he was bad before he left. Worse than when he returned, in a way. That was the difference between them and him.

The Curé's gate opened, and Sister Hermaline stood there. "Monsieur le Curé asks that you all come in," she said.

Hercules Bart, the Town Crier and Constable who had been standing there all the while with his great voice silent, motioned a signal with a swing of his arm to those who had wandered off to the Place.

Slowly entering the garden, the people saw the Curé seated in his canvas chair, his hand on the shoulder of Guichard, who sat beside him, head still bowed. The outcast man looked more like one in deep grief, or mourning, than in shame. And everybody seemed to feel better that he appeared so, for it would have been unbearably embarrassing to look upon shame.

After the gate stopped tinkling and closed on the last, silent straggler, Father Ambrose turned to Marc.

"Tell me, Marc Bracessac," he asked softly, "why did you attempt to save this man's life?"

Marc was nonplussed. "I don't know, Monsieur le Curé," he answered haltingly. "I don't feel that anyone should kill himself, or anybody, I suppose."

"Why not? You have seen carnage. As a soldier you must have become used to that?"

Marc's face clouded. He didn't like to be reminded of things. But he struggled with himself to give the priest an answer. "I didn't ask myself, Father Ambrose. I just acted. I guess it was because life is sacred."

Father Ambrose thought a moment. "Good," he said, in a matter-of-fact tone, "we begin then with a truth. Now we shall have to face a few facts. Very harsh facts. Difficulties . . . difficulties from years back. I will not go into them, except to ask those of you who were boys and girls at the time our neighbor here was a boy, to ask you to search your memories and your conscience. I think you will conclude that Arsac produces not only her own grapes but also her own troubles." He stopped to cough, and Sister Hermaline handed him a glass of water.

Danielle perhaps of all the young people present knew what he meant. Thérèse's picture of Porky's childhood, an ugly little orphan, picked upon by everybody at school, came back to her mind.

"And lest any of you," the priest continued, "should feel individually guilty, let me tell you that this is but another kind of community vintage, a bitter one, in which we have all had a part."

There were scattered nods of agreement.

"Well then, let us come to the more recent difficulties," the priest continued, in a tone as businesslike as though he were speaking on the Executive Committee about the bills to be paid. "Our neighbor here found himself up against one that had him beaten. He and his wife were facing destitution. But in disgrace, and that is the worst kind. He felt the disgrace was not hers but his, and that without him she'd find her way back to our goodwill, as she was already doing when he returned. So he had one solution. Armand," the priest said gravely, "this is for you to tell."

Guichard hesitated. "My wife has had to depend for food upon charity from the Château," he muttered hoarsely without lifting his head out of his hands. "She had to beg. No man can stand that. I've got some insurance in her name. She's been a fine wife and I thought the best thing I could do was to put out the light. The insurance could do her more good than I can ever. The trouble I'm in I brought on myself. I blame nobody else. That's all, I guess."

The priest took a moment before he broke the solid quiet of the company. "We now come to the difficulties before us. You men know that if you hadn't had certain heavy jobs to tackle in the past, you'd never have developed enough strength to do the work you now do without even a grunt? Our neighbor Marc Bracessac, for instance, came back with an atrophied arm. But by making that arm attempt the difficult, he is bringing it back to life, and less than an hour ago he saved a man's life. The spirit gets strong by the same process, tackling the difficult hardships."

Felix Dassier nodded vigorously to Pierre and Danielle, as if to say, see what I meant?

"Now, Armand," Father Ambrose said gently, "I wish you to lift your head and attempt the first great difficulty before us."

Again Guichard hesitated, but he took a deep breath, and turned his haggard look upon Marc.

"When you came into the store, Marc Bracessac, some months ago," he said in a low-pitched tone, "and asked me for work, it was to taunt me, to show me up among the customers. You knew I wouldn't give you a position, even without your disability, because—" he turned aside a second to summon more will to force himself— "because of what I had done. And I knew you wouldn't work for me. It was just to show me up. And it did."

He looked down into his hands. He coughed to clear his throat. "Now," he said, looking up again, and with a fainter voice but higher pitch, "I will ask *you* for a position. But I mean it. And it is not to show up anybody. Now will you, Monsieur Bracessac, let me work for you?"

The astonished Marc turned to look at Danielle.

"All I ask," Guichard pleaded, "is work as a roustabout. I will bring the stock from the freight station. I don't ask you to trust me—"

All eyes had turned with Marc's upon Danielle. Father Ambrose nodded to her. "Speak, Danielle."

All she could do was think aloud. "We all have lost something through the storekeeper," she began. "Only in one case, which happens to be my family's, has anybody got any of it back individually. So my right to speak of this is not the same as it would be for you others. But if you will let me speak for the community I can say we have had restored to us much more than was taken. And Monsieur Guichard has lost everything, more than many of us put together. At the Co-op we are in great need of help. He is the only experienced groceryman among us. He can be as much help to us as we, I hope, can be to him. That's all I have to say, Monsieur le Curé."

The priest stood up. "You now have before you, my friends, your difficulty. It's not a bit pretty. Neither for Armand Guichard, nor for the rest of you."

He raised his hand, and all heads bowed.

When he had left the garden, Mme. Hourdebaight straightened up. "Gentlemen," she said, "this is a matter for the Executive Committee. I invite you to my house."

The gate bell tinkled and in came Thérèse Guichard. She beheld the scene with astonishment. Evidently she had no idea of what had happened. As she moved slowly toward her husband, who drew up his shoulders bracing himself to make things easy for her, the crowd tacitly decided to leave. As people passed Thérèse Guichard, some patted her hand, and some her arm. Danielle clasped her hand. "It will be all right, Thérèse," she said.

16. *Danielle and Marc*

THE ARSAC year was now about to touch its high point socially. The entire village was out with its best foot forward, and an outsider would have wondered where all the finery had been cached. Upon the three converging roads at the Place de la République, little boys and girls walked importantly, wearing portions of the vestments which had been bought for their First Communion. Bigger boys grouped at corners, making sheep eyes at the girls but ashamed to be caught at it. Girls in skimpy bright dresses, by threes and fours, threw back their heads in an abandon of merriment, making sure out of the corners of their eyes that the boys were noticing. Others wheeled their bicycles in pairs down the center of the road, flirted their braids, cried meaningless witticisms to other groups. Into the shade of doorways, elder women, their knobs of hair coifed in black foulards, drew their chairs to barter news.

In the Co-op, not yet moved to the new quarters, the

weekend afternoon was the busiest of days. The sixty members had a feeling of ownership: they came in, trickled the seed grain through their fingers, sniffed the sulphur and superphosphate, discussed new articles for the Committee to add to the stock. And each one felt conscientious about not withholding his own two-cents worth of advice. Danielle bustled among the customers with the right word for each, and a warm feeling that all was as it should be.

True to his proposal, Guichard brought stock from the freight station, using Agathe's donkey cart. He spoke rarely to anyone and never smiled, but seemed content to be let alone to do his work. If anyone spoke to him, he answered in a quiet few words and went back to his job. People let it go at that, knowing his trouble would take time to mend.

In Committee meetings and in the store, with Danielle and Marc, however, he was more natural. He was meek but open-faced.

"Well now, what do *you* think about this, Armand?" Victor would ask from the Committee table.

"It is customary to place orders for that stock along about December," he replied in a tone of not being an authority but wanting them to feel welcome to what he knew, "but putting in an October order pleases them, because it gives them a chance to estimate how much spring business to prepare for."

So those around him began to feel hopes of some day getting to like him really, as Danielle and Marc sized up the situation. They were thankful, at least, for the amount of work he relieved them of.

But she let out a sigh of weariness and relief as she turned the key in the store on that second Saturday night of the vintage. People, with their pay safe in their pockets, had none but good words for her Community Vintage. She had worked hard, but tonight she would forget responsibility and just have fun at Mme. Lescure's ball.

As she brushed out her hair, glad it was still thick and long, she sang as if she had never known a moment's hardship. It was a lavender-and-gold twilight, with the moon coming up through the pines.

Marc came wearing a new white shirt. His blue-serge suit was at last fitting him well. "Now *I* have an idea," he said. "You'll be eighteen in two weeks. To get married, the banns have to be posted in the mayor's office for three weeks. Let's get your father to put them up tomorrow. Nobody will be surprised."

He was quite right about that. During the intermission at the ball—the largest Arsac had ever known, and the most dazzling—M. Bergeron clapped his hands for silence. The people sitting about with paper plates of dainties on their laps, paused in their laughing and eating.

"Ladies and gentlemen," he said sonorously, and in all France you couldn't find a general or statesman more distinguished-looking than Diane's father, Arsac's M. Bergeron. "I have the honor of proposing a toast. To the one who had the most to do with starting our Co-opérative Agricole, whose idea it was to have a Community Vintage, to which this evening's festivities are a fitting climax, Danielle Dufour!"

A great applause arose. Everybody stood up. M. Bergeron held up his hand.

"I can't think of anyone to whom our village owes more than to that girl of Pierre's, who by the way, will soon renounce that delightful title for one more mature. I am asked to announce that tomorrow she will have her banns put up in the town office. Here's wishing you a long and happy life, our Danielle and Marc!"

There was an incredible noise of clapping hands, whis-
tling, and girlish shrieks of joy. All Arsac seemed to descend
upon the Bracessacs and Dufours at once. Mathilde and
Agathe flew into each other's arms. And never before had
such happiness shone on the faces of Jeanne and Pierre!
Jeannot and the other children, as soon as they had learned
the meaning of all the ado, capered wildly. Marc scowled
and chuckled in turn. Danielle reeled but kept smiling.
Kisses, handshakes, pats, hugs from every side. There was
no escape. Dancers ringed them in. Impromptu duets and
quartettes serenaded them. Only early morning and utter
sleepiness finally ended it.

Next morning, the two Guichards appeared at Mass
together. They sat in their usual place. Afterwards, outside,
Arsac again came up to the Dufours and to Agathe and
her handsome grandson to congratulate them. Waiting at
the outer edge of the throng, the Guichards at last came
up and shook hands. "I wish you every happiness," said the
unhappy man, but his wife raised Danielle's hand to her lips,
and said, "May you be spared more than anyone else in the
world any mar to your life."

In the afternoon Marc and Danielle went out to have the
first look they had a chance to get of the Dowry Field since
its return. To them who knew the meaning of land it was
a beatific sight. Here they would grow food for themselves

and their children. They would plant every meter of it. So they talked not in terms of a single crop but in terms of a generation, as they sat under the live oak tree.

"I wonder if there shouldn't be a row of poplars along the Lorina there to hold the bank?" Marc said.

"Decidedly. And we ought to dig a ditch to drain that low left corner," Danielle put in. She was interested also in experimenting with "that new forage crop from China, what's it called?"

"Soy. Soy bean."

"That's it. And don't you think it wouldn't be asking too much if we politely requested our neighbor to the east there to trim back his young pines? They cast too long a shadow, and what gives stamina to the vegetables is the early morning sun."

"Yes?"

"Everybody knows that."

"I think it's a superstition," Marc opined.

"So?"

"Yes, but I want you and the vegetables to have all the sunshine that daytime can give."

She felt his arm around her. It was his right arm, and it was strong.

"Thank you, Monsieur," she said.

About the Author

Robert Davis, born in 1881, lived an energetic and adventurous life spanning two world wars that had dramatic impact upon international relations—an impact that he was personally and philosophically very concerned about. His life seemed to have begun more or less routinely when he chose to train at Dartmouth and Union Theological Seminary, and so become the fifth in his family line to serve as a Vermont Congregational minister. After pastoring a prominent church for ten years, he began a remarkable journey that would add the tasks of humanitarian, overseas reporter, librarian, farmer, teacher, lecturer and author to that of his role as Christian minister. In 1917, during World War I, he was appointed Commissioner for the American Red Cross in France, Austria, Hungary, Armenia, the Baltic States and Europe. Then, from being head of the American Library in Paris, he went on to become an editorial writer, correspondent and reporter in 31 countries. His first wife, Louise, with whom he had two sons, died in 1919.

Remaining in France, Robert Davis later married Kathleen Johnston and together they raised three daughters while living on a dairy farm and vineyard estate in southern France near Bordeaux, the location of *That Girl of Pierre's*. When World War II began and France fell to the Nazis, Mr. Davis fled through Casablanca and escaped to the United States. He resettled in Middlebury, Vermont where he was soon teaching at Middlebury College and was later acting president. His wife and daughters were able to join him in 1942.

Drawing upon his years of varied experiences with people and places, Robert Davis began to write books for young people. His grandson, Gardner Davis, recalls, "For a while he was writing practically a book a month, 14 or 15 of them. Eleanor Roosevelt, the First Lady, was giving gold medals at this time for the best children's book of the month. My grandfather won 8 of these medals." Meanwhile this man, whose humorous, optimistic personality is evident in all his writings, was also a popular speaker.

A short biographical sketch of Davis in an earlier book reveals a key to the upbeat philosophical tenor of his books and of his life: "Robert Davis has been guided by two rules: to pay cash. To drop a job the minute it ceases to be fun." These rules, lived out with what seemed to be typical energy and initiative, are also reflected in the stories set in the distinctively varied and well-delineated locations of his books, showing a universality of experience whether in Spain, North Africa, France, Canada, or New England. The theme of economic cooperation (so we can "pay cash,"—a form of social justice and a ticket to freedom) is set forth in a particularly engaging manner for youth. It presents in concrete terms Davis' thoughtful answer to the questions raised by Soviet communism. He had seen first-hand, in his East European travels, what was wrong with their collective experiment. Irrepressible characters like "that girl," Danielle Dufour, embody Davis' ideals, and, in their confidence amidst difficult circumstances, show us, just as much today as then, what is *right* with the world.

And modern readers may be glad indeed that Robert Davis found it *fun* to write books for young people, thereby sharing with ongoing generations the fruit of the eventful and meaningful life he so energetically lived for others.

Young Adult Historical Bookshelf

TITLES IN THIS SERIES